Praise for Avery Beck's
For His Eyes Only

"Like a great piece of lingerie, For His Eyes Only tempts and teases. It's a sensual delight made enchanting by Avery Beck's signature charming characters...I've quickly come to adore Ms. Beck's stories for their endearing characters and steamy-hot love scenes; For His Eyes Only has both in spades."

~ *Joyfully Reviewed*

"With pulse pounding romance, a sweet story of personal triumph, and a cast of secondary characters that give an uncanny sense of realism, FOR HIS EYES ONLY is an excellent read from start to finish."

~ *Romance Junkies*

"For His Eyes Only is mesmerizing, intense, and at times made me want to weep and scream at the characters that truly came to life on the page...My hat goes off to Ms. Beck who knows how to create a story with a touch of reality that keeps the reader begging for more. If you're looking for a book that will warm the heart, challenge your sense of right and wrong, and provide enough hot, scorching sex to set your soul on fire, then For His Eyes Only is the book to read."

~ *Whipped Cream Reviews*

Look for these titles by
Avery Beck

Now Available:

Sexy by Design

For His Eyes Only

Avery Beck

A Samhain Publishing, Ltd. publication.

Samhain Publishing, Ltd.
577 Mulberry Street, Suite 1520
Macon, GA 31201
www.samhainpublishing.com

For His Eyes Only
Copyright © 2010 by Avery Beck
Print ISBN: 978-1-60504-813-0
Digital ISBN: 978-1-60504-686-0

Editing by Tera Kleinfelter
Cover by Tuesday Dube

First Samhain Publishing, Ltd. electronic publication: November 2009
First Samhain Publishing, Ltd. print publication: September 2010

Dedication

To JJ Sup, for endless support of my career, believing in me even when I don't, and providing the Three C's of Writing that have gotten me through seven manuscripts.

Mom—you don't have to dig through the trash to read my stuff anymore.

Chapter One

Sometime between the decision to take a drink and the act of getting his mouth on the glass, Alex Vaughn's face had ended up between the sexiest pair of legs he'd ever seen. An unexpected elbow had jammed into his back and sent him careening forward, and for a moment, his position near the floor put her ankles at eye level. He let his gaze linger on the columns of sleek, cream-colored flesh that descended from a heavenly place above his head all the way down into a couple of strappy black stilettos.

He didn't dare look up for fear of an angry five-inch heel connecting with his eyeball, but the scenery in front of him made him long for this party to end so he could get on with the reason he attended the damn thing every year. Contrary to what the other employees believed, he wasn't there to kiss up to his father.

That was how he spent every *other* day.

A shiny black toe nudged him in the shoulder. "Go ahead and look. You've seen it all before," it said.

Alex rubbed his temple and picked up his crystal champagne flute, taking a moment to remind himself that shoes didn't talk. Maybe he should have passed up that last drink. He straightened to his full height and a woman's mouth came into view, glossy and red and smirking at him with unwavering confidence.

His reason. She had arrived.

"We meet again." He lifted the glass to his lips before remembering that its contents had splattered all over the carpet, narrowly missing his brand new Ferragamo loafers.

Not that he cared much about overpriced footwear, but appearance meant everything at Insomnia's annual black-tie soirée. Everyone from the chief executive to the newest salesgirl received an invitation to the August bash, and those who weren't rich were still expected to look that way. As the CEO's son, Alex could afford his designer suit, but at the moment all he could think about in regards to his clothing—and his companion's—was the quickest way to take it off.

He took the woman's arm and moved over to allow the hotel staff to clean up the mess. She raised a brow at him, her pale blue eyes twinkling.

"One too many?" she asked, nodding at his empty drink.

White-blonde curls tumbled over her shoulders and onto her breasts, and Alex burned to rid her of the black dress every female in the room seemed to be wearing. Even so, there was no chance this lady could disappear in a crowd.

With a chuckle, he dropped the glass onto a waiter's passing tray. "Actually, someone bumped me from behind. But I'm grateful to that person, all things considered."

He slid his gaze down her legs and back up again, imagining what could have happened if they had been alone in the room when she'd first approached. He would have raised himself to his knees and skimmed his palms up the length of her thighs, then pushed that short skirt aside and found out if she was wearing something from Insomnia's latest collection.

Mesh and lace, black and red, however mixed or matched, those styles currently defined the bestselling items at Miami's most popular lingerie chain. Alex knew firsthand that his mystery woman looked hot enough to melt a mirror in whatever lingerie she chose, and she tasted even better underneath.

She licked her lips at his innuendo, then sipped her glass of red wine before walking it back to the bar, knowing he would follow her. He'd follow her to Timbuktu if it meant he would have a chance to run his hands over every inch of her skin and end up deep inside her lithe, naked body.

"So." She faced him and took his tie between her thumb and forefinger, slowly massaging the silk. "Are you finished playing Mr. Importance? I feel like getting out of here."

"Not tired of me yet?"

"Are you kidding? This is my Christmas morning. The one day a year that I get everything I want."

Alex groaned softly as she circled her fingers around his wrist and leaned close to him so he could smell the hint of vanilla on her skin. He lowered his voice. "You know, I still don't know your name, or what you do at this company."

"You like it that way."

"Well, it is...intriguing."

"The only reason I know your name is because your daddy always preaches to the press about the upcoming exchange of power. You guys ever going to finish that deal?"

He rolled his eyes. His father liked to *tell* everyone that he proudly anticipated his son's rise to the executive position. In reality, William Vaughn's excuses for postponing his retirement grew more far-fetched every week.

The last thing Alex wanted to think about was the long, hard fight he'd have to endure for his promotion. He raked his fingers through those soft curls and whispered in the woman's ear. "If you didn't know my name, what would you scream every year?"

She threw her head back and laughed, a pleasant sound that revealed the relaxing effect of the wine and her readiness to move the celebration to his hotel suite. "You're going for a world record, Vaughn. Can you make me scream your name four years in a row?"

"I can, and I'm willing to prove it."

She grabbed his hand. "Then let's—"

"Alex!" A familiar but unwelcome female voice called to him, and his hand was empty again.

His assistant, Kim Starr, rushed to his side. "There you are. I've got to talk to you. *Alone*," she added with a pointed glare in the direction of his acquaintance.

The fire in his blood doused for the moment, he excused himself and joined Kim in a secluded corner of the room. He wanted to blow off her request as one of her schemes to get him alone and eventually into bed, but the edge in her voice concerned him. His impending promotion had put Insomnia on the radar of entertainment journalists all over the city, and if there *was* a problem, he'd do well to take care of it.

"What's the problem, Kim?"

"I just talked to the photographer who's shooting our summer catalog next month. We've lost our top model."

"Stephanie? She quit?"

"Mr. Vaughn fired her because she's four months pregnant and it's starting to show."

Alex pressed his hand against his forehead. He had just seen the supermodel last week, and for the first time since her *last* pregnancy, she hadn't looked anorexic. But his dad didn't appreciate a woman's natural shape unless the smallest thong in stock slipped right onto it.

"All right, let's not panic," he said, though he couldn't deny her statement lit a spark of queasiness in his stomach. Insomnia prided itself on the summer catalog, which always boasted a world-famous cover model. As Vice President of Corporate Image, Alex was responsible for the final product— and without Stephanie, the company's largest marketing effort would be screwed. And so would his promotion and the only chance he had to take back what he and his mother had earned.

Screwed. The thought pushed his gaze back to the blonde beauty waiting for him at the bar and the ways his body would be tangled up in hers if Kim hadn't chosen this moment to give him news that could wreak havoc on his career.

He had to have her.

The added stress of Kim's announcement only made his heart pound faster and sent his libido through the ceiling. He needed release, and he needed the woman who always provided it with exceptional skill on this night.

He didn't know her name. Whenever he asked her something personal, she changed the subject. He didn't mind the lack of conversation too much, because words wouldn't do justice to the language her body spoke to him. When she'd made her first appearance at the event three years ago, they'd exchanged a heated look that had led to sneaking into an empty restroom and having sex on the counter between the sinks. The next year they'd done it in the backseat of his Mercedes, and last year he had finally taken her to the king-size bed in his hotel room.

They were strangers who had no contact during the rest of the year. But every summer, they met at the party and fell into bed—or onto the nearest available surface—for unbridled, anonymous sex. It had become somewhat of a tradition, one so alluring that he intentionally attended the party alone.

"Listen, Kim, I'm very busy right now. Let me get back to you—"

Her brown eyes flashed. "Busy? Are you joking? Alex, this is a priority. If we don't have a model—"

"We'll have a model. I'll make some phone calls tomorrow and this will be a non-issue on Monday."

Leaving her agape behind him, he pushed his way through the crowd, finally regaining precious contact with his companion.

"Excuse me." He nodded to the balding finance guy who'd been trying to pick her up. "My date and I need to go."

Recognizing Alex and his status, the man held up a surrendering hand and wished them a good night.

"No more interruptions." He brushed his lips against her ear and led her out of the room.

They waited for the elevator. She wrapped her arms around his neck and kissed him, a chaste kiss appropriate for the public eye should anyone catch them. But when she pulled back and stared at him, the way her eyes darkened spoke volumes about the *un*chaste activities she expected to take place once they made it to his room.

Thankfully, the elevator doors closed before anyone else joined them. She slipped her arms inside his jacket, and the heat of her touch penetrated his shirt fabric while he pressed her to the wall, thrust his tongue into her mouth and ground his hips against hers.

"Well," she teased when he rested the solid crotch of his pants against her thigh. "I can tell you're ready."

He closed his eyes, his hunger for her made almost unbearable by the taste of sweet wine she left on his lips. "Oh, don't worry. You'll be ready too."

He put his hand beneath her skirt and trailed his finger along the satin edge of a soaking wet g-string, smothering her approving moan with another kiss. The ache in his groin intensified.

"I think you're right," she gasped when he let her go.

The doors opened. They greeted an older couple waiting to take the elevator and managed to maintain their composure until the door to his room locked behind them.

Then he couldn't take it anymore.

"I've got to have you," he insisted, expressing the thought that had plagued him all evening. He stepped up behind her and kissed the back of her neck, then lowered the zipper of her dress, his mouth following each tooth as it opened.

By the time he reached the zipper's end, he was kneeling on the floor with the skinny strap of those panties right in front of him, urging him to tear the thing off. But he had just one night a year with her, and he wouldn't end it within the first three minutes.

The dress and the lingerie hit the floor before he had a chance to contemplate his next move. He looked up, managing to catch the mischievous grin on his lady's face before she turned and strode across the room, the silken curves of her ass draped in nothing but moonlight.

He stood, his fingers clenched with the need to touch her. "Where are you going?"

"You'll see."

She opened the French doors that led to a private terrace and disappeared around the corner. "Care to join me?" her voice called through the darkness.

He nearly ran to the balcony, stopping just long enough to pull protection from his pocket and take off his suit. When he found her, she was shoulder-deep in the hot tub, curling her index finger at him.

"Hurry," she whispered. He could see her squirming beneath the bubbly surface.

"You sure know how to make a man crazy."

He sank into the warm water and pulled her against him, relishing the reunion of their naked bodies. The money and power that accompanied his position at Insomnia never left him without a date for long, but this woman was no ordinary piece of arm candy. She charged him like an electric current, and their annual rendezvous was just about the only time he felt like a flesh-and-blood man instead of a corporate puppet.

Without exception, when he took other women out, they immediately brought up his job. Each of them shared a mammoth interest in his money and his ability to discover the next pin-up girl.

But not this one. The woman in front of him was wet, naked, and beautiful—and completely uninterested in his paycheck. He didn't think he'd find a more perfect woman if he could design one himself.

Her fingers entwined in his hair, tugging him from his thoughts. She kissed him with a desperation that seemed to match his and pushed him down until he sat on the tub's ledge, the water swirling around his ribs. Then she straddled his lap.

"I need your touch."

Her words energized him and brought his full attention back to the reason they were there. He dropped his hand under the bubbles, skimming her torso until he found the softness between her thighs and unraveled her desire.

"Here?"

"Alex..." She surged against his chest and her fingernails dug into his shoulder.

"That wasn't a scream," he objected.

"Not yet it wasn't."

He massaged her, increasing the pace of his stroke while she squirmed and begged and then came hard, bucking against him and crying out loud. Still trembling, she shifted in his lap, took his shaft in her hand and rubbed it against her flesh.

"Do it," she urged.

Her pleas turned to moans when he complied, slipping inside her and reacquainting himself with her warmth, her kisses, her cries. When he was lost in the taste and scent and feel of her, once again sharing with her the deepest kind of intimacy, he realized there was one problem with his perfect woman.

He didn't know her, not the way he should. At least she could list some of his basic information, like his position at the company and what his mother had been calling him since birth. He couldn't do the same for her. He knew that if he leaned down and sucked on her nipple right now, she'd come again. And if he gently bit the tender spot on her neck, right behind her earlobe, she'd arch backward and push him further into her body.

It was incredible, but it wasn't enough. Not when he held her so close that he couldn't tell his breath from hers, and when he kept imagining waking up in his bed at home with her beside him.

He anchored one hand on her hip and brushed the other through her mass of platinum curls, the ends wet and clinging to her breasts. "Tell me your name."

She blinked, uncertainty clouding her face. But he looked into her eyes and moved slowly within her, and she relaxed. "It's Jacey."

"That's a lovely name."

"Thank you. Alex." She giggled, then gasped and held tightly to him as he began to thrust harder. Her hips matched his intense rhythm, and he broke into a sweat caused by more than the temperature of the water.

At last, he knew her name. The feeling of making love to *Jacey* instead of *that woman* launched his arousal into overdrive. Waves splashed over the sides of the tub while she rode him, and he was vaguely aware of their passionate shouts echoing in the hot, black night.

The spa's acrylic surface became uncomfortable after one round, so they went inside and made use of the huge bed. He buried his hands in her hair and sank deeply into her body, content to watch her expressions as the last remnants of his champagne buzz turned to the euphoria of sexual pleasure. With every thrust a groan rumbled in his throat, each motion threatening to take him over the edge until finally, with him short of breath and her clawing at his back, one took them both.

His pride surged when she screamed his name, but he also felt a sense of comfort now that he knew the identity of the woman who spent so much time in his thoughts even though they rarely saw each other. He made a mental note to learn her job title—and a lot more—before next year.

Something clicked in his mind as he studied Jacey's arching figure and considered her employment at Insomnia. Her full breasts, narrow waist and slim legs, the ecstasy on her face...not to mention that gorgeous hair. She looked like a Playboy centerfold. Draped in lingerie, she'd look like a photograph—a beautiful photograph selling sexy intimate apparel.

As if on cue, she opened her eyes and smiled at him, and he kissed her lightly on the lips before letting her rest and heading to the bathroom to dispose of the condom. He looked in the mirror and grinned at his messy hair and a face that needed a shave. Maybe he *would* find a new model by Monday.

He hurried back into the bedroom, hoping to catch her before she left. "Jacey, can I ask you—?"

He cut the question short when he saw her stretched out on the bed, lying on her back just as he'd left her. For a moment he stood there and listened to her heavy, even breaths. With a smile, he tugged his boxers back on and rested his head on the vacant pillow.

He would ask her tomorrow.

Jacey Cass bolted upright when she saw that she still lay in bed next to Alex in his hotel suite. It didn't take long to notice the bright border the rising sun had painted around the curtains on the window.

Dawn.

Panic swept the air from her lungs. If he woke up and found her there, they would have to engage in morning-after small talk, which would lead to questions about who she was, where she came from, what she did for a living...

God, no. Her skin grew clammy and she pushed the sheets aside, then slid off the bed and crept across the room to collect her scattered clothing. She couldn't give him answers to those questions. He was her escape from all that, and she'd

19

successfully avoided the getting-to-know-you discussion each year. She had no intention of changing that now.

Her heart raced. She fastened her bra inside out and heard the painful sound of her too-tight dress ripping at one of the seams, but she didn't have time to care. Stumbling into the bathroom and closing the door to confine the light, she hurried to shimmy her ankles into the scads of tiny straps on her shoes. It wouldn't be easy to run away in stiletto heels, but she had no choice. She hadn't exactly packed an overnight bag. She and Alex *never* spent the night together.

She swung the door open, flung her evening bag over her shoulder and turned to leave.

A tall, dark, and very familiar figure loomed in front of the exit, arms crossed and expression amused. "Let me guess. An important meeting at six a.m.? On a Sunday?"

Jacey leapt backward in shock but managed not to squeal. Instead, she stuck her chin in the air and studied the expensive artwork on the wall. She had no idea what those splashes of paint were supposed to represent, but at least they kept her eyes off the sinewy physique she wouldn't have the pleasure of seeing or touching for another three hundred and sixty-four days.

"My schedule is none of your business. The point is that I'm leaving. I didn't mean to fall asleep last night."

Alex shrugged. "It's no big deal."

"You must have worn me out." She tried to force a smile, but she was tired and she'd done enough pretending for one weekend. Fancy clothes, schmoozing with executives, looking like a million bucks when her paycheck barely covered groceries...it was nauseating.

Shame burned the surface of her skin. Alex didn't know that when it came to those parties, she only felt real after he arrived and took her in his arms. As far as he knew, she regularly lived the life of the glamorous woman she portrayed every year. He'd never seen her otherwise. But she had been wrong when she'd told him Insomnia's summer party resembled her Christmas morning. It was more like Halloween.

"Well, Jacey, I can see you're in a hurry. I'd like to ask you something before you go."

Her fingers tightened around her purse strap. Did he want to see her again—*this* year? Dating a corporate golden boy would put an end to her financial troubles, but no matter how desperately she needed the cash, she wasn't about to spend her life depending on a man to support her. Her mother's mistakes had taught her the consequences of that kind of idiocy.

"I'm listening," she answered.

"You're familiar with the summer catalog, of course. One of our models dropped out at the last minute and I'm wondering if you might be interested in the job. You're absolutely beautiful, and you would be compensated..."

He talked on, but his words slurred together as her mind began to spin. Could this day get any worse?

She shouldn't have told him her name. She hadn't planned to, but last night had blown away her plan, not to mention the definition of passion as she knew it. Sex with Alex had been great every year—he'd never left her hungry for an orgasm, and sometimes he'd given her enough of them to last through the long months she spent without him. But in the hot tub when he'd asked her name, he had leveled her with a gaze so intense, it seemed to seal a connection between them that went beyond their established physical one. She'd been helpless to deny him an answer, and that was the moment she'd destroyed her plan to stay casual and opened the door to intimacy.

If she were smart, she'd slam it shut. Because now that he knew her name, he'd want to know more. And the more he found out, the more he would try to give her—like this modeling job. Her experience in front of a camera went as far as the photo on her driver's license. How in the world did she qualify to have her picture pasted all over Insomnia's most widely distributed print ad?

She didn't. And unlike her mother, she wasn't touching anything she hadn't earned.

"Stop." She held up her hand. "Just stop."

"Is something wrong?"

His concern tugged at the vulnerable corner of her heart. She considered curbing her sarcasm, but she had to put some distance back between them before she blew her cover. She didn't want his money or his pity, two things he'd inevitably offer if he discovered the pathetic truth about her life.

She stabbed her finger in the direction of the window. "When the Winter Olympics are held on South Beach, *then* I'll be your model."

He paused, then quirked an eyebrow at her. "A 'no' would suffice."

He looked confused, even hurt, and she felt guilty for snapping at him. Of course he wouldn't understand. A man as rich as Alex, with even richer parents, would have no idea how appalling it was to grow up with a mother who traded sex for grocery money and waited for handouts to buy everything else. It wasn't his fault she had to override that legacy by accomplishing something that required a brain.

But that didn't take away the sting of his request.

The shrill ring of a cell phone stabbed into her pounding head. She raised her hands to her ears.

"Who would possibly be at the office today?" Alex mumbled. He crossed the room to take the call and indicated they would continue their conversation in a moment.

Swallowing another pang of guilt, Jacey waited until his back was turned, then quickly left the room. Her throat closed up and her feet carried her down the hall, onto the elevator and through the ornate lobby. That last image of Alex lingered in her mind—his tousled dark hair, the muscles that defined his bare back and his hand cradling the phone. She wished she could touch his hand one more time, or at least say goodbye.

But she couldn't. She had royally screwed up when she'd fallen asleep last night. She had crossed the boundaries of their fast-and-furious sexual arrangement, not only risking her anonymity but giving him the opportunity to insult her with his modeling offer. On top of the fact that she didn't want him handing her anything, she was a hypocrite. She'd insisted on keeping their relationship casual, yet she resented the possibility that he might not think of her as anything more than a potential pretty face for the catalog.

When she was locked inside her car with the engine humming, she rested her forehead on the steering wheel and gave in to one tear. Okay, two. But she swiftly wiped them away, then stepped on the gas and zigzagged through the parking lot before merging onto the highway. She was so tired. Her emotions would surely settle down as soon as she curled up in her own blankets, closed her eyes and forgot about this disaster of a morning.

Ten minutes into her mad dash home, she noticed a flash of silver growing larger in her rearview mirror. She squinted and adjusted it. What in the world...?

Abruptly, she changed lanes. The silver car followed her. Cursing her ridiculous heels, she pressed the gas pedal down and thanked heaven for the absence of traffic. The speedometer rose to eighty, then eighty-five. The other car had more power and rapidly caught up to her.

She glanced at the mirror again.

Alex?

He was in the driver's seat, flashing his headlights at her and jerking his thumb toward the side of the road like he wanted her to pull over. *Like hell.* First he'd tried to recruit her for a job with no basis for doing so, and now he was tailgating her like a crazed stalker. His record of sexual prowess and irresistible charm suddenly didn't seem so flawless.

A quick glance over her shoulder confirmed that the right lane was clear. She launched her car to the opposite side of the highway, barely making it onto the exit ramp that would take her home.

Her phone rang—surprising, since she hadn't paid the bill and her service provider had threatened to disconnect it last week. With any luck, the police would be on the other end of the line.

"Hello?"

"Jacey, please stop the car."

"How did you get this number?"

"I have access to any information you listed on your employee application."

"And I suppose you regularly use that information to your advantage." He was still following her as she turned onto her street.

"No, I don't. I need to talk to you about the job. Reconsider my offer. I'll give you anything you want in return."

That's the problem, she wanted to scream. "Let me think about it for a minute. *No.* N-O."

"Jacey—"

"Look, I'm not who you think I am, okay? There's nothing glamorous about me. I'm a freaking salesgirl, Alex. I make minimum wage. Now get off my back. And my car."

Unwilling to lead him directly to her apartment, she hung up, parked in front of the main office and waited for him to leave.

He brought his car to a stop just short of entering her apartment complex. When she looked out her window she could see him sitting there, watching her. Their eyes met. She shivered at the memory of the way those eyes had looked at her last night.

This was the reason she never spent the night with Alex. When she woke up in her own bed, their rendezvous seemed like nothing more than an erotic dream. He was not supposed to be part of her next-day plummet back to reality. He wasn't supposed to see that she rented an efficiency instead of owning a nice house, and she didn't want him to know that she stocked inventory and worked a cash register every day instead of sitting at a desk, typing away on a computer and making important phone calls.

But now he knew everything, and their four-time fantasy wouldn't see a fifth.

A strange feeling of sadness settled deep within her. She took one last moment to remember the scent of sweat that had lingered on his neck every time she'd buried her face there while he thrust inside her. She imagined the thrilling sensation of his warm, bare skin against hers. Then she met his eyes again and shook her head in a silent ending to whatever it was they had shared.

He stared at her for a minute, his expression solemn, and then drove away. Jacey sighed as though releasing every last memory of him through her lips.

Chapter Two

"I want the sexiest women in this city in the ballroom at the Ritz-Carlton on Friday."

Alex walked slow circles around the long, narrow conference table. Insomnia's corporate staff scribbled furious notes on their legal pads as he spoke, and even his father sat listening to his instructions. He held back a triumphant smile at the knowledge that soon, he'd wield this much power on a regular basis.

The colossal project he was about to introduce would save the catalog, catapult the company into the public eye and prove his ability to handle anything the business might throw at him. How many people could design an entire modeling competition in half a day? For thirty-two years he'd been "William Vaughn's boy", but this media event would turn the tables. When he took the company reins, people would be saying *his* name. Preferably with a sir attached to the end.

"Think Miss America meets American Idol," he continued. "Except we won't drag this out over several months—we'll have our winner *next* month. Three weeks, thirty contestants. Ten women get cut after the first and second shows, then our finalists compete on the last day when the winner will be chosen."

Kim Starr stuck her pen in the air. "How do you suggest we handle the voting?"

"The old-fashioned way. Ballots and a box. We'll collect ballots from the audience after each show. The auditorium seats fifty-eight hundred, and that's enough to decide which contestant will bring in the highest profit as our new model."

He scanned the table of nervous faces. "I realize we're working on a tight schedule, but you've seen the crowds of gorgeous ladies out there on the beach who have no qualms about showing off their bodies. We'll have no trouble finding our Sleepless Siren in time to shoot next summer's catalog."

"Excellent work, Alex." His father rose from the executive chair at the head of the table and glared at each employee in turn. "You've got four days to market the hell out of this competition. Make it happen."

Upon hearing those trademark words of dismissal, everyone but Alex rushed from the boardroom, undoubtedly back to Sunday dinners the emergency meeting had interrupted. He planned to dump after-hours conferences once he was in charge. Weekends existed for a reason, and if he ever had a family life he didn't want it compromised. His dad's excessive office hours had filled his parents' relationship with bitter arguments and cold silence. Two years ago, his mother had finally left.

His father's powerful lawyer had made sure she didn't take any part of Insomnia with her, even though they'd both founded the company. She'd spent years working night and day to help his dad turn Insomnia from a unique small business into a celebrity-frequented hot spot, only to walk away with a meager settlement. She swore that the stress reduction she'd experienced since being on her own satisfied her, but Alex wasn't so easily appeased. Since he was a child he'd aspired to inherit the business, and that's exactly what he planned to do—and then he would give back the holdings she deserved.

William stuck his hands into his pockets and sauntered to the floor-to-ceiling window behind the conference table, watching the sun set on the Miami skyline. "This is our chance, Alex. If we pull this off, even Victoria's numbers will look like small change compared to our sales."

He groaned inwardly at the determined tone in his father's voice, not to mention the impossibility of his statement. Insomnia boasted plenty of designer merchandise and enjoyed wild popularity around town, but Miami was only one city. The company had never been in the same league as the industry bigwigs, but his father still insisted on competing with them. He wanted national recognition and would stop at nothing to get it—and the profits it promised.

"I have to admit, son, I'm impressed. You might find yourself in charge of this place yet."

No kidding. Alex was counting on that.

He'd made dozens of phone calls that afternoon, but of course every supermodel on the planet had already been booked. That discovery hadn't disappointed him too much, because he didn't believe any of their overexposed images would create the unique, breathtaking fantasy that Jacey would as the focus of the catalog.

There had to be another woman in the city blessed with that same exquisite beauty. This competition would not only find her, it would get Insomnia's name all over the state and maybe beyond before simply hiring a model ever would.

"Make it soon, Dad. You've already ignored your doctor's orders for three months."

His father cleared his throat and then turned his back on him. "That isn't your concern. Now go, I have work to do."

Alex shook his head, leaving the office and closing the door behind him. Actually, it was his concern. His dad had been diagnosed with heart problems due to stress, and his doctor as well as the Board had recommended that he step down. But the man was stubborn, and Alex often suspected he valued his company more than his own life. He didn't seem to care if his health suffered, he'd let his marriage go to hell, and Alex would be damned if the two of them had ever played catch in the backyard or had a couple of beers together at the end of a long day.

He headed down the hallway toward his own office, trying to remember if he'd thrown a bottle of Tylenol in his briefcase before he had left his condo. His issues with his dad weren't helping his head, which felt like someone had been playing drums on it since Jacey had run from the hotel early that morning.

It pained him that she'd turned down the modeling job. He couldn't understand the ice that had hardened in her eyes when he'd mentioned it. Most women who could boast that kind of striking beauty started knocking down the doors of modeling agencies as preteens. But Jacey was unique, and judging from the dismissive look she'd given him from her car, he wouldn't have a chance to know her beyond the handful of mind-blowing encounters that had already taken place.

What rotten luck. The night he'd managed to make some emotional progress with her, she'd bolted—not exactly the reaction he expected from a woman who came at least twice each time they got together. A dull pain weighed down his chest at the prospect of never seeing her again. Or worse, seeing her at the next party without being able to touch her. Or seeing her on the arm of some other guy.

Oh, hell. He was in deep, and he hadn't even seen himself fall.

He collapsed into the chair behind his desk and found the Tylenol, then grabbed a bottle of water from a drawer and swallowed half of it in one gulp. When he opened his eyes and saw Kim standing in his doorway, he suspected it wouldn't be long before he would need another dose.

"Hey there." She crossed her arms beneath her breasts, boosting the visible cleavage at the center of her blouse. Alex was certain her shirt had been buttoned to the top during the staff meeting. "Got a headache?"

"I'll be fine. It's just been a long day. Aren't you going to head home?"

"Well, I thought you might want to get a bite to eat, since we're the two singletons around here."

"I appreciate the thought, but I really can't. This competition has buried me in work." He hoped Kim would take the hint and let him be. Instead, she strutted closer to him and leaned her hip against the side of his desk.

Her fingernails traced the buttons on the cuff of his shirt. "You know, things have been kind of awkward between us lately. Is everything okay?"

He rubbed his eyes. He was running on three hours of sleep and his day had been a chaotic mess. The last thing he needed was a sermon about their one-time affair, which had happened years ago when he'd had a bottle of vodka and enough ego to enjoy playing the role of spoiled playboy. The moment he'd awakened from that nightmare, he had parked their relationship back at *friends*—he was her boss, after all— and vowed to stop being such a womanizer before he got himself sued for harassment.

"I'm dog-tired, and my career depends on the success of this modeling contest. Other than that, everything's fine."

"So I guess you couldn't get hold of her?"

He blinked. "Who?"

"What's-her-name—Jacey. When I called this morning about the meeting and you asked me to get her number from the database, I figured it was an emergency. Something to do with the model situation, I'm assuming."

"Thanks for getting the information for me. But no, I couldn't reach her."

Wasn't that the truth. He turned to his computer and tried to work, but Kim's eagle eyes unnerved him. Just as he opened his mouth to ask her to leave, she pushed off the desk and gave him a little smile.

"Well, then. Just let me know if you need anything."

"I will. Thank you."

When she was gone, he took another swig of water and pulled up the employee database on his screen. He didn't make a habit of digging around in the staff's personal information, but the desire to know more about Jacey was driving him mad. Despite the way she'd blown him off this morning, he couldn't accept that his curiosity may have come too late.

As a rule, he tried to keep from getting attached to any particular woman. Most of them were looking to seduce their way into a photo shoot, and he figured he'd spare himself the disappointment. But now he knew modeling wasn't on Jacey's agenda, and seeing her more often made for an appealing possibility.

He typed her name into the search box and her file popped up, complete with a color photo that looked like it had been taken at the DMV. She was smiling in the picture, and gorgeous as ever despite the notoriety of bad license photos. He'd never seen her face so many times in one year, yet after the way she had run away from him, he felt farther away from her than ever.

He scanned the contents of the file. She'd told him the truth on the phone this morning—she worked for minimum wage as a sales associate in a nearby shopping center. But of all the facts revealed in that file, her birth date shocked him the most. She was only twenty-four.

He conjured up an image of the way she always looked at Insomnia's parties. He could picture her down to the last detail, and while he understood that she probably made herself up quite a bit for those evenings, something in addition to her looks had made him believe she was closer to his age. She exuded independence and maturity, not to mention a level of sexual abandon unmatched by even his most experienced past lovers. He certainly hadn't taken her for a girl barely out of college—or one who hadn't attended at all.

The scene in the parking lot came together in his mind. Their encounters at each party had been filled with mystery. They'd known very little about each other and because of the staggering difference in their salaries, Jacey had preferred it that way. Now that he knew there was nothing glitzy about her true identity, she planned to hide from him.

But there was one advantage to being at the top of the social ladder—Alex got what he wanted. And he wanted Jacey badly. He would see her again, and it would happen long before next summer.

Jacey dropped the black dress and sorry excuse for a pair of shoes onto the sales desk in a series of thuds.

"Sorry I'm so late returning these," she blurted when her friend appeared behind the counter. "I'm trying to save gas, and there's a tear in the dress and I haven't had a chance to—"

"Hey, hey, relax." Monica Valdez stashed the garments out of sight, then reached out and put a hand on Jacey's shoulder. Concern filled her soft brown eyes. "No biggie, sweetheart. What's the matter? Party wasn't any fun?"

"Oh." With a sigh of pure longing, Jacey closed her eyes and envisioned Alex in his sophisticated suit, then pictured him *out* of it. "The party was great. As usual."

"So you did see him!"

She couldn't help returning Monica's excited grin. The woman was old enough to be her mother, but she had never married. She believed men made better toys than companions. Monica dressed like she could be asked to enter a nightclub at any given moment, and she made a fortune designing and selling sexy, eccentric clothing out of a boutique in Bal Harbour.

A simple walk through the beautiful array of high-end stores made Jacey feel like she hailed straight from the ghetto.

Which, essentially, she did. Her mother's run-down trailer park certainly wouldn't attract the urbane crowd that strolled past the shop windows, as much a part of the scenery as the lush palm trees and tranquil ponds.

"I saw him, all right. All of him."

"Yum. So why the long face?"

She shrugged, her heart clenching at the way things had ended with Alex. She had spent the past week mourning the loss of their yearly tryst, having realized how much she'd always anticipated it only after the possibility of another one was gone.

"He asked my name," she finally said.

Monica stared like she was waiting for news a bit more disturbing. "So?"

"So it means he wants more. He wouldn't need to know my name if we were just getting together for a booty call once a year."

Monica clasped Jacey's hand between both of her manicured and jewel-adorned ones. "Honey, that's great. From what you've told me, he sounds like a prince."

"Exactly. I don't need his glass slipper to save me."

Her friend's eyebrow arched in an authoritative manner that reminded Jacey of the kind of mother she wished she had—one who worried about her life and the direction it took. "Please don't tell me you're not going to see him because he makes a lot of money."

"That's not the only reason," she insisted. "I'm not sure he's different from any other guy, really. He just thinks I'm cute."

"You know that's not true. He can have any woman he wants at those parties, and he picks *you*. Every year."

"He asked me to model for Insomnia."

Monica paused, the silence broken only by the clinking of the bangles on her wrists. Jacey braced herself for a lecture. Flaunt-it-while-you've-got-it Monica didn't see anything wrong with making a living on one's good looks. She regarded that as a dream job, while Jacey considered it a nightmare.

The two of them were polar opposites, but there wasn't anyone in the world she loved more than Monica and her seventeen-year-old daughter, Danielle. A decade ago, when she was young, alone and had nowhere to go, Monica had taken her in and paid her to be a nanny to Danielle as well as do some administrative work for her budding business. After graduating high school she'd moved out on her own, but she had remained in close contact with the Valdez women. They were the closest thing to family she would ever have.

When Monica spoke, her voice was gentle. "You're quite the looker, honey. Why is that so surprising?"

Jacey pressed her lips together and inspected her shoes, old athletic ones that almost made her miss the excruciating but stylish stilettos. She wished she could be so nonchalant about the whole thing. Ultimately, Alex had offered her a job, and she needed money more than anything in the world.

Wrong. She needed self-respect even more than she needed money. Being "quite the looker" wasn't the skilled accomplishment she had in mind.

"There's something else, isn't there?"

She looked up. "What?"

Monica folded her hands on top of the counter. "I mean, this is about more than wanting to earn your own money. Other people have offered you jobs before—*I've* offered you a job before—and I've never seen you get this worked up about it. So what's really bothering you?"

The woman read her like a book. And she was right. Jacey was used to declining help, and if a stranger on the street had offered her a modeling job, she'd have walked away and gotten over it.

But Alex, the source of the most powerful pleasure she'd ever experienced, was no stranger. A naïve part of her heart had dared to believe Monica's earlier assertion—he *did* pick her every year, after all. She had almost believed she was special. His blatant request to use her body for profit had proven her terribly wrong.

"I don't know, I just...I thought he saw more in me than that."

"You see each other once a year and you spend that time having sex. What would—"

"I know, I know. I guess I felt like he knew me. That probably doesn't make any sense."

Monica smiled and adjusted the top of her sequin-trimmed tank, a shirt suspiciously similar to one she had just given Jacey. She didn't want to take advantage of Monica's financial success—that was one of the reasons she'd refused a permanent job at the boutique. But that didn't stop Monica from presenting her with a stack of clothes every few months, insisting they were old things that no longer fit. Yet the two women wore the same size, and the items looked way too trendy and new to be hand-me-downs or garage sale fodder.

"Sounds to me like you want to know him outside of the bedroom. Why don't you spend some time with him? Go on a real date?"

"Don't be ridiculous," Jacey scoffed. "We have nothing in common. He only likes my body and I've known that all along. Hell, I like his body. I *love* his body. It's the only reason I go to that stupid party."

Monica leaned forward, clearly not buying the cavalier attitude. "Are you sure about that, hon? I thought I was the poster girl for casual sex, not you."

"Oh, I'm no poster girl. It just seemed okay with Alex. I don't know." She waved her hand and crossed the room to study a scantily-dressed mannequin, uncomfortable with the sadness that once again crept into her chest.

That stuff she'd told Monica about liking Alex's body wasn't entirely accurate. True, he had muscles she'd like to lay her hands on permanently and a grin that could melt steel, not to mention a hefty package that had never come close to disappointing her. But his tenderness, his ability to make her feel like a virgin in her true love's arms at last, had brought her back to the party year after year.

She could feel Monica staring at her. "You know, Jace, if Alex is really a good guy, he's not going to be bothered by your past. And he probably is a good guy, or you wouldn't feel so strongly about him."

"I don't feel strongly about him," she snapped, even though Monica would see right through her lie. But Alex was money. He was power. Regardless of how he made her feel, he was everything she had never been and everything she refused to depend on for survival. She pushed an unwelcome image of her mother out of her mind.

The doorbell chimed, signaling the entrance of a customer who would distract Monica from psychoanalyzing her. She breathed a sigh of relief and dug her keys out of her pocket, prepared to jump on the opportunity to escape.

"Hey, Mom. Jacey! What's up?"

She looked up at the sound of her name, pleasantly surprised to see that the newcomer was not a customer but Danielle, who had just begun her senior year of high school.

"Hey, Dani. How was school?"

"Great. Have you seen this?" She waved a sheet of paper in the air. "I think I'm going to enter. You should too. You'd win for sure."

Win? Her curiosity piqued, Jacey studied the flyer, but her hopes fled as she read the bold letters at the top of the page. She handed it back with a little laugh. When it rained, it poured.

"Sorry, but a modeling contest isn't for me. You should definitely go for it, though."

Danielle gawked at her. "Not just *any* modeling contest. A contest sponsored by *Insomnia*. The winner gets a year-long modeling contract, their picture on the front of the summer catalog—"

The older women shared a chuckle at her breathless excitement. Jacey put a hand on her friend's shoulder, studying her dark hair and exotic brown eyes.

"I know it's a big deal, sweetie. Like I said, go for it. You'd have a great shot at winning."

Danielle poked her fingernail at the bottom of the flyer. "And a hundred *thousand* dollars! Hello? Who wouldn't enter? Except you," she teased.

Jacey barely heard her. Her mind had stopped processing words when she'd heard the amount of the prize money.

"One hundred thousand? Are you sure?"

"Totally. I read it a million times. Everybody at school is talking about it. Man, I could get a sweet car and a penthouse apartment or something."

Monica plucked her daughter's backpack from the floor and gestured toward the back office. "Well, until then, go do your homework. Just in case you don't win."

Playfully, Danielle stuck her tongue out and headed for the office. Monica shook her head and smiled, shooting Jacey a wry glance.

"You know…"

"No. Don't even say it."

"She's got a point, Jacey. You could win."

"I could humiliate myself. In front of Alex, no less."

"Alex thinks you're beautiful."

"And I already told him I didn't want the job."

"He won't care if you change your mind." Monica stepped closer and offered her the flyer, compassion in her gaze. "You're not your mom, honey. You deserve this. That's a whole lot of money they're offering."

She bit her lip. It certainly was a lot of money. Enough to get her through school, and definitely enough to get an apartment in a safer part of town. Maybe even enough to start a freelance media planning business after she earned her degree. How many years had she been nursing that pipe dream?

But none of that mattered. Monica had it right—she wasn't her mom. She would not accept payment from a man she'd slept with. No doubt Alex's offer hadn't been one of prostitution, but the scenario was similar enough to make her uncomfortable.

"I can't do it," she muttered, then made a quick exit before Monica could talk her into it.

She got into her car, which refused to start until the sixth turn of the key. Not for the first time, she worried that the clunker she'd bought in high school was on its last leg. Yet another reason she could use that prize money.

One hundred thousand dollars. The words taunted her, the possibilities making her head spin.

But to win the competition and therefore the money, she'd have to sport tiny lingerie in front of a whole lot of people. Whenever she thought of putting her body on display so blatantly, she imagined the way her mother used to strut half-naked around their mobile home. Drunk, or high, or both—and giggling hysterically while her latest boyfriend groped her, neither of them paying any regard to Jacey's presence in the room.

Ugh.

She made it to her complex without any further mechanical problems, then trudged up the stairs to her apartment, still clutching the contest flyer in her hand as though it *were* the hundred grand. God, that was a lot of money. But she wanted to go to college and sustain a career, not strut down a runway and profit from her cleavage.

Her mind made up, she crumpled the flyer between her fingers, intending to toss it over the rusty railing. Her fist froze around the paper ball when she neared the top step and saw a notice pasted to her front door.

No. It couldn't be.

She ran the rest of the way up and tore the sheet from the door, frantically scanning the words. *You are hereby notified that your tenancy of the following premises will terminate—*

Horrified, she stopped reading and jiggled her key in the lock. She'd missed rent a couple of times, but she'd explained her financial troubles to the lady in the management office. Where was the leeway she'd been promised? Had it been more than two or three months?

Her heart sank as she realized the answer. The raise she'd been waiting for at work had never come, and she'd fooled herself into believing she would improve her situation before she missed another payment...and another and another.

Inside, she sifted through a stack of mail, tossing the junk and filing away the bills she couldn't pay. Then she sat on her bed and stared at an envelope from the University of Miami. Maybe this was her year. If so, she'd avoid the humiliating fact that not only hadn't she made any progress toward her goals, but she'd taken a step backward by losing her apartment.

When she opened the flap and pulled the letter out, one glance at the first line told her it wasn't good news. Once again, the school had denied her a scholarship.

She tore the letter to shreds and watched as the tiny white bits floated around and landed on the carpet. Slowly, she unfolded the contest flyer and smoothed out the wrinkles, her gaze latching on to the amount of the prize money. Prancing around in her bra still didn't appeal to her, but she could no longer afford to be picky.

She had thirty days to escape her mother's fate.

Chapter Three

The Ritz-Carlton Ballroom resembled a backup location for teenagers whose Spring Break had been rained out. Giggling women filled the place, most of them appearing to attend high school or college. Cleavage abounded and tight clothes left no curves to the imagination. It was exactly the kind of senseless scene Jacey had envisioned.

She filched a brochure from the display table, rolling her eyes at the bikini-clad woman pictured on the front and the same headline that had screamed at her from the poster in the display window at work. *YOU could be next summer's Sleepless Siren.*

She had zero interest in being next summer's Sleepless Siren. Her stomach churned at the very thought of signing a document that would legally bind her to such a job. But the contract only lasted for a year—that wasn't so bad. She'd been through worse, and tough times called for tough decisions.

She pulled a compact mirror from her purse and smiled at it, adding powder to her nose and crimson to her lips. The thought of breaking away from generations of hardship strengthened her resolve, and she pasted on her most confident smile as she pranced through the crowd, stopping at the first of two sign-up tables. She guessed this one was responsible for weeding out the girls who didn't have a chance, because she'd already watched several of them run away in tears.

"My name is Jacey Cass," she announced to the bespectacled guy behind the table. "I bet you a hundred thousand dollars that I'm the Sleepless Siren you're looking for."

"You and everyone else," he mumbled, not looking up.

Well, *everyone else* wasn't quite as determined as her. Insomnia's staff had set up a dozen floor mirrors in the room, and girls practiced their poses in front of each one. Jacey suspected none of them would be out of a home and an education if they didn't win the competition.

"Here, take a number." The guy handed her a sheet of paper while his gaze raked over all the places it shouldn't. "And fill out this form. They'll call you over to that table when they're ready for your audition."

"Thank you very much." Fighting nausea, she gripped the ticket that labeled her as wannabe number four-oh-two. She'd read on Insomnia's website that audience voting would decide the winner, and that was the only thing saving her sanity. Convincing a few thousand people she looked good in a teddy might not require genius, but it was still more proactive than having Alex slip the contract into her pocket after sex.

She smoothed her hair, startled at the tremor that awakened her body when she thought of Alex and sex at the same time. Hadn't she told Monica she was done with that fairy tale? In fact, if she won the contest, she would leave her customer service job long before next summer's party. She'd never see him again.

She was still wondering if she'd dropped her heart into a meat grinder forty-five minutes later, when a woman's voice called her number over the loudspeaker. She ambled over to the second registration table. The dark-haired woman manning that station held out her hand to take her information sheet, then glanced up and frowned.

"Weren't you at the party last weekend?"

Surprised, Jacey studied the woman's face—she was the guest who had dragged Alex away from Jacey just as things had started heating up between them. Since it ended up being her last time with him, she thanked her lucky stars the woman's plan to interrupt their night together had failed.

"Yes, actually, I was," she answered.

The woman—Kim, according to her name tag—snorted. "I'll have you know that the winner of this contest will be chosen by a public audience, not by Alex."

"So?"

"So don't expect your special favors to him will help you today."

Jacey fumed. Here was another reason she needed a degree—so people would quit assuming she was a dumb blonde without any nonsexual skills.

"Alex doesn't even know I'm here." She didn't bother to add that if she got her jobs through special favors, she'd be on the cover of the catalog already.

"Uh-huh."

"Will you please fill out the paperwork so I can finish my audition?"

Kim made a show of going over her entry form as slowly as possible, then jabbed her finger toward a curtained-off corner of the room. "Fine. Go have your fun, but this game you're playing won't work. Alex is a professional, and he's here to do what's best for Insomnia."

That caught Jacey's attention. "Alex is doing the auditions?"

"*If* the three judges behind the curtain think you have the right look, you'll go to Alex for final approval. Like you didn't know. Do you really think he's going to put you through just because you're easy?"

Her condescending laugh cut through Jacey's chest. *Easy.* Until she'd met Alex, she hadn't particularly liked sex. In high school, it had been a thirty-second event designed to get the guy off. As a kid, she'd associated it with men bigger and older than her who reeked of pot and pedophilia.

She had no clue as to the identity of her father and she was certain her mother didn't, either. She only knew that when she was fourteen, her mom had brought yet another stranger into the house, but this time she'd insisted Jacey was old enough to start contributing to the household.

Just the memory of that man made her shiver. He'd had greasy hair and a stained shirt...and he had smelled horrible. When he'd focused that predatory look on her while her mother stood there smiling, she had run away as fast as her feet would carry her. Thankfully she'd met Monica, and she had never looked back.

She didn't intend to start now. This competition could make or break her future. Nothing, not Kim and her jealous wisecracks or Alex's attempted handouts, would stop her from earning the win.

Muffled, angry voices sounded on the other side of the partition wall that separated Alex's part of the ballroom from the main audition area. He welcomed the distraction. The leather-clad redhead dancing in front of him couldn't have been more than eighteen, and he could hardly bear to sit through another performance. The competition's minimum age limit was seventeen, but it seemed everyone had mistaken that number for the maximum. Where had the over-twenty segment of the population disappeared to?

He wanted an adult—a hot, sultry, provocative *woman.* Someone his customers would dream of being. Someone whose image would inspire other ladies to buy Insomnia's lingerie so they too, could feel that damn sexy.

The young girls, though attractive, weren't cutting it.

The redhead flipped her hair. Again. "So, what do you think?" she asked, changing back into her street clothes.

Alex produced the fabricated smile that, after six hours of use, had begun to hurt his face. "Lovely. Thank you. We'll call you tomorrow if you make the cut."

The girl beamed and rushed off. He sighed, hating to think of all the entrants who would sit by the phone for the next twenty-four hours, only to end up crushed by its silence.

He heard a couple of women scuffling again—probably another fight between a pair of best friends, only one of whom had made it into the competition. He got up from his chair to see what was going on, but someone opened the door that joined the rooms and got to him first.

His heart rate increased tenfold when he identified the woman standing there.

Jacey. Was he seeing things?

No, he'd recognize that cloud of blonde hair anywhere. Like something out of his dreams, the two of them were alone, her gaze locked onto his in silent acknowledgment of the intimate ways they knew each other. The piercing blue depths reminded him not only of what he wanted to see in a contestant, but of the four blissful nights he'd spent exploring her body.

He fought to regain the function of his brain. "Jacey, hi. What are you doing here? Not that I'm not happy to see you."

In fact, certain parts of him were a little too happy to see her, and that could very well interfere with his objectivity as a judge.

"I'm here to audition, of course." She smiled, but she crossed her ankles and then uncrossed them again, as though she couldn't get comfortable. "Lucky for me, the judging panel likes me better than the woman at the desk. Why are you picking the contestants? I thought that would be some assistant's job."

"I wanted to do it myself. It's very important to me that this contest is a success."

Briefly, her eyes dropped closed, and he'd swear she said, "Me too."

Was she serious? Why she would rather audition for the contest than accept his personal invitation to do the catalog shoot?

He crossed his arms. "I offered you the same job this competition is promoting. Why didn't you take it?"

"I take care of myself," she answered immediately. "I don't want charity."

His mouth opened in disbelief. If he wanted to know more about her, he'd just learned his first lesson. She was stubborn as a bull.

"Charity? I offered you a job. A paying job."

"It was a job you were going to give me because you think I look good in bed. A lot of chicks look good in bed, and a lot of them want to sleep with you. Go shower them with your generosity."

He stepped closer, intent on showing her the truth—she meant a lot more to him than some cheap one-night stand. "I don't want anyone else," he told her, his voice low.

She held his gaze, and desire darkened her eyes. But when he reached for her, she moved away, determined to state her case. "Look, I'd be an idiot to pass up the kind of cash the contest is offering. But if I win, then I win fair and square because people voted for me. Not because I gave the VP a blowjob."

Her statement stunned both of them into silence. Alex stared at the wall behind her, inexplicably hurt by her tawdry description of their nights together.

"All right, then. Have it your way." He gripped his clipboard and returned to his chair.

His heart continued to pound at the nearness of her body, and he was suddenly grateful he wouldn't be the one choosing the winner. He had a responsibility to do right by his company, but Jacey's refined eroticism tended to drag his thoughts away from brand recognition and profits. In fact, he had already marked her down as one of the thirty contestants.

But it certainly wouldn't hurt to see her audition.

He assumed his most professional tone. "See that X over there on the floor? Stand over there and show me what you've got. Your body, from all angles. Use the chair too. Let me see your flexibility."

Where had *that* come from? She didn't lack flexibility—he had learned that much during their first encounter on the bathroom sink.

She struck a pose that turned his knees to jelly and made him thankful he was sitting down. She looked fantastic. The miniskirt and high heel combo showed off her long, lean legs, and a sheer camisole revealed her narrow waist and sexy navel.

Those red lips shone at him again, and her hair tumbled down her back to form a profile that could only be compared to a goddess.

Unsure which head was doing his thinking now, Alex hurried to the second part of the audition. "You need to wear lingerie. You can use your own or we've got a rack over there to choose from."

She laughed. "You want me to strip?"

Boy, did he ever. But he just said, "Yep." That's why he had a private room. The first round of judges scored on figure, face and hair, a test Jacey had no doubt passed with flying colors. Once a woman made it to him, it was his job to decide if her bared look was worthy of a cover shoot.

She considered his request, then shrugged. "Okay, but shame on you for forgetting what my body looks like—in *and* out of lingerie."

"Oh, I haven't forgotten."

He had memorized the surface of her skin to the point that he could almost taste it. The vision had provided him with quite a few instances of self-satisfaction, but his hands were a poor substitute for Jacey. Just the thought of seeing her body again made him ache in ways he wouldn't be able to relieve for far too many hours.

She approached his chair, then slid her hands over his shoulders and down his chest. "Well..." she whispered in his ear. "In case you need a refresher."

She stepped back and peeled her shirt off. He stared, motionless, while she ran her hands down her torso, her hips gyrating in a slow, painful tease. He shifted in his seat. He'd been watching women do this all day long, but something about the way Jacey moved...

Her skirt slipped down her legs and hit the floor. She stood before him in Insomnia's newest, hottest bra set. Skimpy. Red. And absolutely transparent.

He tried hard to remain professional, though it was nearly impossible given the look in her eyes. She was no longer performing for the audition, but for him.

"Jacey—um—you don't have to show me quite *that* much."

She stuck a shoe on each side of his legs and straddled his lap. "I thought you wouldn't mind."

The fruity scent of her long, curly mane wafted into each breath he took. When her mesh-encased nipples prodded his shirt and he imagined the soft patch of blonde hair pressing into his groin, the last of his bureaucratic intentions scattered.

"I don't." He tossed his clipboard to the floor, then plunged his hands into her silky hair and kissed her until his cock grew painfully rigid with need.

She threw her head back so he could move his mouth down her neck. "Alex, do me a favor."

"Anything." He moved against her, burning to get out of the mobbed ballroom and into his condo, where they could be alone and he could make love to her all night. Her skin was smooth and hot beneath his tongue, and he vowed not to let her get away a second time.

Her shaky whisper brushed his ear. "Take me one more time, because I can't see you again."

Kim Starr tapped her pen against the growing stack of entry forms waiting for Alex's attention. They only had an hour left to choose three more contestants, but she knew that Alex had already picked the winner in his mind.

51

For seven years she had been his assistant. She used to want him—she'd had a few drinks with him at a Christmas party a few years back and, finally, he had accompanied her home. But he hadn't spoken to her much since then unless he needed her to run an errand, and her attraction had waned.

Now, though, that one night they'd spent together proved vital to her success in getting the information William had asked for. Alex still believed she wanted him, and his mistake provided her with the perfect cover for taking an interest in his personal life. He would blow off her curiosity, assuming she was just nursing a crush on him.

"Excuse me, are the rest of us going to get a chance to audition or what?" A reed-thin brunette stood on the other side of the table, her hands on her hips to punctuate her demand. "I've been waiting all evening."

Kim stopped her pen mid-tap, taking a long look at the girl who bore a striking resemblance to her younger sister. She sighed. The second anniversary of Katelyn's death was right around the corner and Kim had been seeing her face everywhere.

"Let me see what's going on."

She rose from her chair and walked to the opaque curtain that blocked off the audition area. She was about to call Alex's name when she peered around the edge of the fabric and saw the blonde slut from the summer party sitting on his lap, nearly nude, with her mouth attached to his.

She dropped the corner of the curtain and put a hand to her mouth to conceal her grin, her stomach flipping somersaults. William was going to love her when she told him about this. She could hardly believe her luck that the woman had showed up for the audition. She couldn't have planned it better herself.

"You're next," she announced to the brunette when she returned to the table.

The girl nodded, then turned away to continue waiting.

Kim couldn't stop watching her. The girl's thick hair fell straight to the small of her back, just the way Katelyn's had...and the way Kim had worn her own hair until she'd chopped it to shoulder-length after the accident. What she would give to get her hands on the brainless bitch who had been behind the wheel of that car.

It was disgusting, really, the way a half-witted beauty queen could get away with anything if she showed enough skin. The sorority princess who'd run the stoplight and killed Katelyn had gotten off with a fine and a few months of community service, despite the fact that she'd been driving with more alcohol in her system than a brewery. And now there was Blondie, thinking she could make the big time because she sexed up Insomnia's second-in-command on a regular basis.

Feminine laughter floated out from behind the curtain, and Kim cued the brunette to make her entrance. Then she rifled through the entry forms until she found the object of Alex's affection. She ripped a Post-It note from its pad and scribbled down the girl's name and other identifying information. Then she dug her phone out of her purse and made the call.

It rang twice. "William Vaughn."

Kim smiled. "Hey, there. I've got all the proof you could possibly need."

Chapter Four

Alex rubbed his neck and stared out the window while his father examined photos of the Sleepless Siren semi-finalists. He had picked some stunning contestants, but his dad's disparaging eye was working overtime as usual. He heard mumbles after each flip of a page, comments like "bad hair", "too fat", and "too old".

Suddenly the room fell silent, prompting him to turn away from the incredible view of the ocean and face his father's desk. The inspection had come to a halt. A grin crinkled the corners of William's eyes while he bent close to one of the pictures. Alex stepped closer to see which girl had managed to garner approval, and the sight of Jacey in that scrap of a bra filled his mind with blazing memories.

"I want her," his father said.

Don't we all, Alex thought, yet a shock wave of jealousy put his senses on alert. He didn't appreciate the sight of his dad leering at a woman half his age—a woman Alex felt belonged to *him*.

"You've got her, Dad. She's one of the thirty and I'm sure she'll make it to the top ten."

He shook his head. "No."

"No, what? You don't think she'll make it? Have you seen her full-length—"

"No, I mean the top ten isn't good enough. I want her to win." He stood up and whistled softly, still staring at Jacey's image. "This girl is a beauty. Customers will flock to our stores wanting to look like her. Yes, I'd be thrilled to see her get that contract."

Alex narrowed his eyes. He hated that devious tone in his father's voice. Dear old Dad was always looking for a backdoor way to increase his revenue—another reason Alex needed that promotion, and he needed it soon.

His father's business knowledge and dedication had made Insomnia into a huge success, and for that, Alex admired him. But that success had gone to his head, and now he treated the company like a resource for his own benefit. Alex couldn't wait to change the place back into a welcoming outlet for women's fantasies, the sensual experience his parents had originally intended it to be.

"So would I, personally," he said. "But that's up to the voters."

William looked up from the photo and pinned him with a domineering stare. "Not anymore it isn't. It's up to you."

"What?"

"You heard me. I'm much more qualified than the public to judge what's best for this company. She's our Sleepless Siren. Make it happen."

He dropped the picture into Alex's hands and turned his back. Alex studied Jacey's features and almost forgot that his father had just suggested they threaten the integrity of the competition.

Almost.

He shook his head and followed his dad to the opposite side of the office. "Wait a minute. Are you asking me to fix the contest?"

His father spun, anger deepening the creases on his forehead. "I'm not asking you anything. I'm *telling* you." He snatched the photo back and held it up. "She wins, and this office will be yours by the end of the year. If she doesn't win, then neither do you. Is that clear?"

Alex clenched his fists, tempted to stick one in his mouth to keep the names he wanted to call his father from being spoken aloud. His head hurt again, which wasn't surprising since the reality of the ultimatum had struck him like an eighteen-wheeler. His competition, the project he had designed to inject life into the dictatorship that Insomnia had become, would be nothing more than another one of his dad's single-minded decisions. A farce.

And Jacey, who had emphasized the importance of winning the contest on her own merit—what would she think of this asinine plan? *If I win, then I win fair and square because people voted for me. Not because I gave the VP a blowjob.*

He winced at the memory of her impassioned words. She would hate him, no doubt. But unless he wanted to throw away his shot at being named CEO, there wasn't a damn thing he could do to change his father's mind. He had to think about his mother and the future of Insomnia. He had to win back the company, whatever the cost.

"As a bell," he growled.

He stalked out of the room and headed for the elevator. Thankfully, it was lunchtime. He was tempted to take the rest of the day off—either that or buy stock in Tylenol.

But first, he had to take care of one more thing. He and Kim had contacted twenty-nine of the contestants over the weekend, to the tune of ear-splitting shrieks and profuse butt-kissing. But his attempts to call Jacey's cell number had only produced recorded messages saying the number had been disconnected. If she had changed it to avoid him, she'd forgotten that would leave him no way to get in touch with her about the details of the contest.

Not that he minded making the drive to her place. They had business to discuss that had nothing to do with the competition—namely, why she'd insisted they go their separate ways even while dripping wet in his lap. She was a complex puzzle, one he didn't intend to give up on until he solved.

He didn't have her address with him, but he remembered most of the streets they'd driven the morning after the party, and he used familiar landmarks to guide him the rest of the way. He drove several miles into the east end of town, still cursing his father.

No one wanted Jacey to win that contest as much as Alex did. Her powerful marketing appeal was one thing he and William did agree on. But whatever her reasons for entering, her reaction to his original offer had told him just how much she wanted to earn the job herself. She would kill him if he manipulated the results in her favor.

Maybe he could explain it to her someday, after they knew each other well enough to deal with the complexities of their respective families.

First, he had to get her to open her door.

He spotted her old Toyota and parked next to it, noticing for the first time how run-down her apartment building was. Most of the exterior paint had peeled away in the heat, and many of the residents' windows were cracked or completely missing. He locked his car, not at all comfortable that Jacey lived there alone. She didn't make a lot of money, but he hadn't expected her situation to be this bad.

He climbed the stairs to search for the apartment number he had seen on her entry form, and thoughts of the audition brightened his mood. Oh, how he had wanted to finish what they'd started behind that curtain. She had kissed him, had reminded him of their roll in the hot tub last weekend...and when he'd reached to unzip his pants and bury himself inside her right there in that chair, he had heard Kim's voice on the other side of the door preparing to send in another model.

Jacey had quickly dressed and gone home, and his balls had turned a dark shade of blue for the remainder of *that* evening.

He found her door and knocked. When he'd questioned earlier if she would open it, he'd been referring to her statement that she couldn't see him anymore. But now he wondered if she'd feel safe enough to come out. He had an urge to stand guard right there in the corridor and ward off unsavory characters.

She must have been used to the place. She answered after only a moment, and the sight of her pretty face and beautiful curls warmed his entire body. She had her hair pulled back and wore minimal makeup along with jeans and a plain green T-shirt, but the way his blood burned every time he looked at her, she might as well be dressed to walk the red carpet.

Her mouth fell open when she saw him. "What are you doing here?"

"I'm here to inform you that you made it into the Sleepless Siren competition," he announced with a flourish. Then he held up his phone. "I couldn't get you on your cell."

She blushed. "Oh...yeah. It's not working right now. I'm having some issues with the service provider."

Issues that involved the bill and her failure to pay it, he imagined.

"Anyway, you didn't have to drive all the way over here to tell me that." She leaned against the doorjamb and changed her expression from alarmed to completely cool. "I figured I would make it."

She flashed him a cocky grin, but it didn't hide the unease in her eyes. At times he suspected she covered up insecurity with overconfidence, and this was one of them. The way she refused to acknowledge her financial situation—which, judging from the condition of her apartment, was probably worse than she'd ever admit—concerned him.

"Well, I needed to make it official and give you some information. Can I come in?"

"Oh. Sure." She hesitated, her smile gone. Then she stepped back and allowed him inside.

It was obvious she had never intended him to come within a mile of her place. He gave her hand a reassuring squeeze when he entered her living room. She shrugged in return and briskly walked away to straighten the pillows on her bed, clearly embarrassed to let him witness her modest lifestyle.

It was then that he noticed her apartment consisted of only one room. The bed she was making stood a few feet from the living room, and if he took two steps to his left, he would be in the kitchen. Clothes and books were strewn across the small efficiency, a place as chaotic and unkempt as her life seemed to be.

His dread about rigging the contest began to dissolve. Jacey needed that money. If he could ensure she received it without letting her in on his secret, she would have no reason to get angry with him—or refuse the prize, which seemed like something an independent woman like her would do.

He cleared his throat in an attempt to break the silence and ease the stilted air between them. He missed the provocative, easygoing woman he'd known at the parties. Did she think he would treat her differently because he made more money than she did?

He reached for a folded piece of paper inside his jacket. Damn, he was still wearing his suit. That definitely wouldn't bridge the gap between them.

"So, the first round of competition takes place on Saturday." He slipped off the coat and draped it over his arm. "You need to be at the auditorium by five o'clock, and this information sheet will tell you everything else you need to know. And of course, you can always call me."

She approached him long enough to take the paper. "Right. With my dead phone."

Ignoring the foot in his mouth, Alex pulled out his wallet and handed her a business card. "In any case, here's the address of the corporate office. I'm on the sixteenth floor. Stop by any time."

She nodded, tossed both things on top of a small TV, and began arranging knick-knacks on a bookshelf.

He scanned her apartment for something to talk about, anything he could say to make her feel better. He noticed scraps of white paper scattered at his feet and bent to pick one up. A chunk of the University of Miami's logo was printed on one of the fragments. Another said admission, and though he couldn't tell if the news was good or bad, he guessed it was bad considering the fate of the letter.

Jacey wanted to be an academic? Wow. She intrigued him more every day, and talking to her more than once a year had made his life more interesting than it had been in...ever.

"Snoop much?"

Her voice yanked him back to reality. He dropped the jagged scrap of paper and found her standing in front of him, her arms crossed like a disapproving parent.

"Uh, sorry. I was just—"

"Uh-huh." She plucked the bits of paper off the carpet and tossed them into a plastic wastebasket.

"I had no idea you were trying to go to college. What do you want to do?"

She beamed at the question. "Media planning. I'm good at math and my years of retail experience have taught me a ton about marketing. I was thinking maybe I'd major in that. I got accepted, in case you're wondering."

So she *had* been accepted. Pride and relief coursed through him. Maybe now she could get her life on track—and move. He couldn't stand the thought of her going to sleep, alone, in the middle of such a dangerous part of town.

"That's wonderful," he said. "Congratulations."

Her face fell as fast as it had brightened. "No, it's not. They accepted me a long time ago, but they won't award me a scholarship. And that means I don't go."

"Why not?"

"Because my grades aren't enough. The scholarship application requires an essay, and I don't write well. I told you, I'm a numbers person."

"I meant, why can't you go without the scholarship?"

She glared at him with outstretched arms. "Does this look like a high-priced condo to you? I can't afford college. I can barely afford to put gas in my car."

She stared out the window at his shiny silver sedan that only made her vehicle look worse. What would she think of *his* high-priced condo? It had impressed the hell out of women he used to bring home for drinks and sex, but without a doubt, it would probably disgust Jacey. She wasn't the materialistic type.

"What about financial aid?" he asked.

"No way. Forget about it."

"Why not? Tons of students do that."

"I told you, I don't want help. I'm not living my life the way my mom—"

She fell silent, then shook her head and walked away. Alex hurt for her, a feeling he wasn't used to at all. He'd been surrounded by wealth and publicity since childhood. What circumstances had forced such a beautiful, smart and spunky woman into near-poverty and isolation, even from her own family? He didn't want to be someone else that faded from her life, so he took the one approach that got them on equal ground.

He left his coat by the door and followed her to the kitchen. She picked up a plate and scrubbed it with more vigor than necessary.

"Jacey, what are you doing?"

"Cleaning. I wasn't expecting company."

"Don't you think that can wait? We can probably find a better way to spend what little time we have together."

She ignored him and tossed the plate to the other side of the sink, then started washing a coffee mug. Her whole body shook with the effort, and her eyes never left the dish.

He caught her arm and pried the mug from her fingers. "Stop."

"What are you—?"

He brought his mouth down, nudged her lips open and entangled his tongue with hers. She smelled of coffee and cinnamon and he tasted his fill, aching to remind her of the desire that had always burned between them. Her body slackened in his arms, and she sounded breathless when he let her go.

"Wow. Is there more where that came from?"

He didn't play along with her attempt to lighten the mood. "I don't care what your place looks like. Do you think I check the economic status of every woman I talk to? You don't have to impress me."

"Who says I want to?"

"You do. You've been acting strange and pushing me away ever since the day after the party, when I found out where you live."

The pain in her eyes lessened the effect of her scowl. She didn't answer him. He wanted to talk to her, find out more about her life and convince her she didn't have to keep her distance because they hailed from opposite ends of town. But his immediate concern, for the sake of his promotion and her financial stability, was the competition. If she couldn't summon her usual confidence within the next couple of days, she wouldn't be able to deliver a performance hot enough to give her the win without raising suspicions.

The party...that gave him an idea. Something about the parties must have made her feel good. During the four times they'd met up there, she'd never given any indication that her life was as tough as what he saw now. She had been a picture of glamour and sophistication. She'd been on fire, and fire would win the contest.

That was it, then. He would do everything in his power to rekindle her memories of their private after-parties. He had to make her feel sexy like never before, or it would be both of their futures down the drain.

Gently, he squeezed her arm, the pressure of his fingers a promise of more pleasurable contact to come. "You're the sexiest woman in this town, Jacey. I can't wait to see you on stage, showing all of Miami what I already know. I want to watch you tease everyone with your beautiful body, and then I want to take you home so you can tease *me*."

Her blue eyes focused on him. For a moment, she looked confused that he'd dropped the subject, but his desire to please her seemed to make her happy. She chewed on her lower lip, a smile threatening. Her fingertips trailed down the side of his torso. A shiver raced through him.

"You want to be teased, do you?"

Her gaze was pure innocence, but the playful tone of her voice suggested otherwise. Not to mention the way her fingers tugged at the waist of his pants.

He released a ragged breath. "Very much so."

In a matter of seconds, she'd lowered his zipper and reached into his boxers. His hands flanked the counter on either side of her while she massaged his swelling cock. When she let him go, he grabbed her waist and hoisted her onto the counter. She made a whimpering noise and curled her legs around him, and he saw the familiar heat return to her eyes before he kissed her again.

Oh, yes. The eager movements of her tongue, her feminine sighs of pleasure...*this* was the woman he remembered. Her long hair moved between his fingers, slipping away when she pulled her shirt over her head and revealed that she wasn't wearing a bra.

"Dear God, Jacey."

He tried to slow down, but he couldn't keep his eyes or his hands away from those hard, pink nipples. Her continuous moaning wasn't helping his restraint, either.

"Suck on them," she cried. "Put your mouth on me."

Her flesh quivered at the brush of his lips. He raked his tongue over the tip of her breast and sucked with as much pressure as he could without causing her pain. She clawed at his head and soon their mouths collided again, his unchecked erection jutting into the denim that blocked him from the warmth of her body.

"You're going to have to get those jeans off."

She squirmed and lifted herself a couple of inches off the counter. "Get rid of them."

He pulled the button open, nearly ripping it off, and caught a glimpse of sleek white material he couldn't wait to get his hands on.

"From Insomnia?" he asked while he fumbled with her zipper.

"No. A gift."

"Oh, really?"

She swatted at him. "Not that kind of gift. Just a friend who likes to buy me nice things she shouldn't."

Thankfully, he succeeded in tugging her jeans down in time to erase the discomfort that had crept back onto her face. What was up with her and other people's money, he might never know. But there was one thing she would accept from him, and he vowed to make it the best thing she'd ever receive, every time they were together.

Which he hoped would be a lot.

He left the denim pooled around one of her ankles and returned to his position between her knees, tracing the satin panties and preparing to pull them aside. He smiled at the look of intense anticipation on her face.

His left hip vibrated.

He glanced down at his pager, which continued to pulse and buzz. He turned his attention back to Jacey, but her eyelids flew open.

"What's that noise?"

Damn it. "Kim's calling me from the office. Don't worry about it."

She turned his wrist and saw the time. "You're on your lunch hour."

"It doesn't matter."

With a shake of her head, she pulled him up and whispered against his neck. "Finish what you started. Do it quick. It's okay."

Air rushed from his lungs. They'd been interrupted at the audition on the brink of making love, and each time they were together, he never knew if it would be the last time he saw her. He wasn't about to leave her with a quickie.

But before he could say that, she kept talking. "I want you inside me more than anything. Definitely more than an hour of cuddling afterwards. You know that. Do it."

Her eyes reflected the same panic he'd seen before she'd left the hotel room last weekend, and the source of her hurry dawned on him. It wasn't the hour of cuddling she wanted to avoid. She figured if they kept their relationship to quickie sex, the way they had before he'd found out her name, she could keep him from getting any closer to her—and her financial problems.

That wasn't going to work. He already cared too much about her to ignore her troubles. And he wouldn't give a damn if she lived in a cardboard box on the side of the road—he was going to spend some quality time with her. Right now.

"Are you rushing me out of here?" he asked.

A deep pink colored her cheeks. "Um—I—"

He chuckled. "Don't answer that. I'm teasing. I have one more thing to do here, and then if you want me to go, say the word."

He had his finger around the satin before he finished his sentence. She stared at him, too breathless to object, which was the point.

Settling between her knees again, he dragged the fabric out of his way and skimmed his mouth over her silken flesh. She inhaled a noisy breath that encouraged him to continue. He kissed her more deeply, moving his tongue inside her and then drawing her swollen clit between his lips until her legs shook and she begged him to stop.

"Should I go to work now?" he whispered.

She shouted something that sounded like a curse. Her nails scratched his back, and she pulled him up and forward. "Go to work on me."

It was his turn to curse. He loosened his tie and ripped it off, so hot for her he'd begun to sweat. He brought her to the edge of the counter and removed her panties, merging their bodies at last.

While they made love, he began to understand Jacey's concerns about the two of them growing closer. Her turbulent life worried him, but he was preparing to take over a hugely successful company. He didn't have time to play the part of anyone's caretaker, and she wouldn't tolerate it even if he did. He'd do well to focus on the solution to both of their problems—her victory in the modeling competition. If he got too involved with her, he'd muck up his father's plan, and his career and her future would suffer as a result.

When he helped her back into her clothes, she smiled and rubbed his shoulders, then kissed him softly.

"Get to work, Mr. Almost-CEO."

He cringed. If she only knew what he had to do to rid himself of the *almost.*

Chapter Five

Jacey's eyes darted around the shop while she processed a credit card payment for the last of what had been a long line of customers. Quickly, she presented the gentleman with his receipt for a black lace garter belt.

"Thank you for shopping at Insomnia. Enjoy your purchase."

The man smiled and nodded, and as he walked away she hoped he actually would enjoy his purchase. He'd been one of the rare ones, the well-dressed guys who visited on occasion to surprise their wives with unexpected romance on a special birthday or anniversary.

Most of her customers weren't like that. She hadn't had the luck of being placed at the Ocean Drive location, which boasted sales to movie stars, record producers and all kinds of people who wouldn't have the least bit of interest in a saleswoman. No, unfortunately, she worked at a mall in the city where average folks dropped by to giggle, buy things they were way too young to be wearing, or gawk at the ridiculously low-cut shirts Insomnia required the female employees to wear.

Today, she'd attracted a gawker. He was beginning to scare her, which was the reason she'd rushed Mr. Nice Customer out. She wanted to go on break, somewhere far, far away. And she wanted to stay there until the weirdo was gone.

He looked about forty and pretended to browse the display of push-up bras he'd been standing next to for ten minutes. His constant staring made her spine crawl. And now they were the only two people in the store.

Her supervisor, a man who was a condescending ass despite the fact that they were the same age, would pitch a fit if she left the desk unattended. She stalked to the back of the shop to find her coworker, a purple-haired high school sophomore who had an infuriating habit of leaving her alone at the register. She found the girl in a dressing room, clutching a lace bustier to her middle and pouting her lips at the full-length mirror.

"Hey, Tyra Banks. Can you help me with the customers sometime this year?"

The girl, Nina Something-or-other, jumped at Jacey's voice. She grinned sheepishly and hid the garment behind her back. "Yeah, sure. I was just checking out the new collection. It's so gorgeous."

Jacey rolled her eyes and headed back to the counter. She'd be doing a similarly annoying act on stage in a few days. Was it really worth it?

Of course it was. She wouldn't be up there flaunting her boobs with hopes of being printed out and pasted to a teenage boy's ceiling. She'd be earning the means to go to school and finally change the course of her life. That was worth anything.

"Whatever," she said, still watching the creepy guy with his hands inside the rack of bras. A snake tattoo curled around his neck.

Nina followed her, the bustier in her hand. "I think my boyfriend is getting this for my birthday," she gushed.

"Great. Let me hang it up so it's available when he comes in to buy it." Jacey snatched the garment from her along with a stack of discarded clothing from a hook on the wall, and she did her best to look engrossed in placing the hangers back on their appropriate racks. Creepy Guy had chosen a silver vinyl costume bra, and with Nina at the register, she could sneak away for her break when he went to pay for it.

Except he didn't head for the register. With the bra in his hand and a sneer on his face, he approached *her*. The hair at the nape of her neck stood on end. She glanced toward the desk, but Nina was on the phone, her back turned.

"Can I help you?" Jacey forced a smile as she returned the last item to its proper place.

"You bet you can."

She sighed, then turned to the guy and crossed her arms, reciting the answer she always gave these kinds of people. "Flattered, but not available. If you'll take your purchase to the front desk, Nina will ring it up for you."

He chuckled, holding the bra dangerously close to her shirt. "Actually, I'd like to see what it looks like before I buy it. You know, I don't want to spend all that money just to be disappointed."

"Well, there it is. You can clearly see what it looks like. If your girlfriend doesn't like it, you can return it for—"

She gasped when he stepped closer and pinned her against a large display of teddies adorned with fur. They were far from the front entrance where mall shoppers passed by, and no one would be able to see her petite frame pressed between all that fluff.

His breath stank of last week's lunch. She nearly gagged. "I don't wanna see it on my girlfriend. I wanna see it on you."

She swallowed, trying to decide whether to scream or kick him in the balls, but her mind was too panicked to focus. "Sir, I'm not allowed to try on the merchandise. Company policy."

"I don't see your manager anywhere around here."

He was right. Her manager had gone to lunch, and Nina had disappeared once again. No other customers were in sight.

Shit.

His stench swirled around her head like a thick fog. He moved even closer, and she shut her eyes as the bra scraped against her chest. He continued to whisper sickening innuendos, but she could no longer make out the words because her brain was flooded with visions of a similar moment that had taken place years ago. She'd been thirteen, and one of her mother's paying customers had followed her into the bathroom.

While she'd been pressed against the closed door, he had groped his fill. He'd gone so far as to put his hand on her mouth and reach for his pants, when her mom's voice had called his name. He'd left, but not before dragging his cold, sticky, ash-tasting lips over hers.

The guy in the store emitted a similar odor, one of smoke and dirty sweat and possible gingivitis. She started to hyperventilate. "Please, I can't—"

She couldn't finish her objection, because his hand grabbed the back of her pants. Her palm struck his face before she could stop it, before she could even blink.

She could breathe again, but only for a moment.

He stumbled backward, stunned, and she saw an angry cloud form in his eyes that told her he might return the assault. She squeezed between his body and the racks and ran for the sales desk, intending to grab her purse and tell Nina she was sick and going home for the day. She prayed the guy wouldn't follow her, and when she turned back toward the exit, she ran right into her manager.

"Larry, thank God you're back, I—"

"What the hell was that?"

She blinked, his accusatory tone stinging almost as much as her hand. She looked from Larry's glare to Creepy Guy's smug smile. Her red handprint lingered on his face.

"I can definitely explain. He—"

"Asked you for an opinion regarding what color would look best on his wife, and you slugged him?"

"*What?* No, I—"

"This is a place of business, Ms. Cass, not a haven for feminist indignation. If you can't handle the sensual nature of this company, I suggest you leave."

So much for asking her boss for help.

"Did you hear me? You're fired. Get out. Nina, see that this gentleman gets a credit on his account."

Jacey's mouth opened. Nina looked at her wide-eyed. She'd stepped out of the back room in time to witness the end of the scene with Creepy Guy, but she just shrugged. They both knew Larry wouldn't believe either of them when his sympathies already lay with the Oscar-worthy performance of the customer.

You're fired. The words congealed in her ears like month-old milk. She stumbled through the shop and out of the mall, blind to the people, shopping bags and garbage cans she ran over in her haste.

She had no job. No income.

The thought haunted her as she ran for her car and tried to steady her breathing, tried to will away the nausea making its way up her throat. She still had the contest. In three weeks, Insomnia would announce the winner.

Three weeks. Even if she found another job today, she wouldn't get her first paycheck by then. She had scraped together most of her last one to pay her landlord a couple of weeks' rent, and she'd used the rest of it to spring for the lingerie she'd worn to the audition. Could she survive three weeks without any money at all? And that was assuming she won the contest. She couldn't entertain the possibility that she would fail.

Her head fell back on the driver's seat. The air conditioner blew hard against her pasty, hot skin, but she couldn't rid herself of the feeling that she was suffocating. Alex's business card stuck out of her open purse and she reached for it, gripping it like a child's comfort toy. She wanted to hear his voice. She wanted to feel his arms envelop her, his touch protect her and his kiss erase her problems from existence.

But she didn't even have a phone. She spotted a pay phone near the mall's entrance but quickly nixed the idea of calling him. What would she say? *Alex, I need you to fuck me until I forget about this hell I call life.* Yeah, that would go over really well.

Besides, booty calls and male saviors weren't her forte. She needed a better plan—she needed Insomnia's prize money.

She headed home. The first round of competition was only two days away. It would end with her image imprinted in the voters' minds, no matter what she had to do to make that happen.

Kim closed the door to William's office, turning the lock until it quietly latched into place. She stared at her hand on the doorknob and released a slow breath.

"You wanted to see me?" she asked.

Butterflies danced in her stomach. She could feel him watching her, and her back began to sweat from the heat of his gaze. With a quick tug at her blouse, she turned to face him.

He sat behind his desk, reclining in his big leather chair with his arms crossed behind his head. A smile played on his lips. He looked at her in a manner quite inappropriate for the workplace, and she briefly wondered if she did, in fact, still have clothes on. But she returned his hungry stare, her mind swimming with rumors she'd heard about what happened in the boss's office after hours...and her body hoping she would be the latest recipient of his affections.

The man was stunningly handsome. It was easy to see where Alex had gotten his good looks. William was fifty-something, Kim knew, but a stranger would never guess. He still had a head full of dark hair, a solid, lean build and deep brown eyes that an unsuspecting woman could drown in. No wonder the tabloids had posted his face all over Miami when he had finalized his divorce. Gossipmongers couldn't wait to name the next Luckiest Woman Alive.

"Yes, I did." His calm, low voice contrasted the sharp-tongued demands he made to the staff every day.

She swallowed. Everything about William's demeanor confirmed her suspicions that this meeting wasn't business-related, and she dared to believe it would be a culmination of the innuendos that had bounced between them over the last couple of days. She'd been attracted to him for years—of course, she expected the same was true of all the women in the office. His physical appeal, power and confidence made for a potent aphrodisiac.

The desire she'd once felt for Alex paled in comparison.

William motioned for her to come closer. "Have a seat."

Her legs shook with every step. She perched on the edge of an armchair, smoothing her skirt and crossing her legs so the material inched up her thighs.

"What can I do for you?" She flashed him her most professional smile, though that was the last sentiment she wanted to hear in his answer.

He sat up straight and rested his clasped hands on the desk. "It seems we have something in common, and I'd like to explore that in more detail."

She squirmed in her chair, aroused by his blatant admission of their mutual attraction and aching to *explore* anything he wanted. She blinked a couple of times and emitted a modest giggle, like a demure secretary should. If William had a fetish for role play, she was game.

"And what, exactly, do we have in common?"

"A desire to take down Miss Jacey Cass."

Her jaw dropped. She uncrossed her legs.

Jacey Cass? What in hell did she have to do with getting laid by the gorgeous company president?

"I—I'm not sure what you mean."

"Mmm. That surprises me, because on the phone you seemed rather excited to out her relationship with my son."

Kim froze in her seat, shocked by his calm accusation. Had it been that obvious? He wasn't supposed to know she was getting personal satisfaction from doing a simple task he'd asked her to do. She fumbled for an explanation.

"You wanted to know if Alex had his eye on any of the contestants. You wanted evidence if he did, and I was just—"

"Tell me what you have against her, and I'll do the same for you."

His eyes still burned into hers. She hesitated, then looked down at her lap before meeting his gaze again. Images of Katelyn's lifeless body flashed through her mind.

"My sister was killed by a drunk driver. Some blonde bimbo on her way home from a frat party."

"And a certain young lady reminds you of this blonde bimbo."

"Yes. People like that should be locked up. Big boobs and a pretty face don't count as contributions to society. I'm sorry if that's inappropriate."

He chuckled. "It doesn't matter. The point is, we're working toward the same goal. I think if we work together, we can get it done more quickly."

"I don't think I understand. What exactly is your goal?"

He stood, slipped off his jacket and draped it over the back of his chair. "I don't suppose you recall the incident a while back, when you walked into my office and caught me doing things some might consider...unprofessional." A slow laugh rumbled in his throat.

Panic washed over her. She'd never forget the day she opened his door and caught him getting friendly with one of the models—one of the youngest models, a girl still in high school. But that had been a couple of years ago. He wouldn't fire her for that...at least, she hoped he wouldn't. Her salary was paying off Katelyn's debts so her sister's young, grief-stricken widower wouldn't have to worry about them.

"I never told a soul," she said. "I promised you I wouldn't. That hasn't changed."

He waved his hand. "You didn't have to. Seems the Board has figured it out on their own."

"Oh, no."

"Yes, well, I've been careless recently. In any case, they're itching to get me out of here and get Alex in before a scandal hits the press."

"Well, um...that seems logical, I suppose."

"No." The palm of his hand came down hard on the surface of his desk. "It's not logical. It's blackmail. And I'm not about to give up *my* company that easily."

Kim had never heard the man so angry and possessive, and it frightened her. But his fury subsided as quickly as it had come. He approached her, offering his hand. Her breath caught in her throat when she took it, rising from her seat and relishing the heady experience of their first skin-to-skin contact. He was so powerful, and so sexy. He ran his fingers through a lock of her hair, and she shivered when he touched the back of her neck.

"Kim, darling, I know Alex never treated you right. My son doesn't recognize quality when he sees it, which is why he will never be in charge of Insomnia. He's only here at all because his mother insisted we include him."

Her heart raced. Her emotions flipped between shock at William's cold manner toward Alex, confusion as to why he was involving her in his personal business, and raw lust.

"Why are you telling me this?" she managed to ask.

"Because, my dear, you have a desire to ensure that Jacey Cass fails to win that competition. And in order to take care of my...complications here at the company, I need you to continue on that path."

She opened her mouth to object, because it seemed like the right thing to do. But William held up his hand.

"Don't ask me questions. We'll talk more about this later. Just promise you will do everything you can to keep her from winning that contest."

She promised. It wouldn't be too hard, considering her sour feelings toward the girl. And now that the man who controlled her paycheck and made her insides quiver had requested it, she was more committed than ever to avenging her sister's death.

But for the moment her mind turned to mush, because William stepped closer and placed both hands on her shoulders. His lips trailed a feverish path along her neck. She reached for him, and he opened the top button of her blouse. His words were a seductive whisper.

"I'll make it very, very worth your while."

Chapter Six

The last time Alex had this much nervous energy, he'd been sixteen and having sex for the first time. The small room packed with gorgeous women in negligee might have had something to do with the rumba taking place in his stomach. Maybe it was the fact that his future, as well as his mother's and Jacey's, depended on the success of this night.

Or else he was trying to figure out how to keep his cool when Jacey walked onto that stage half-dressed, because he'd barely slept since the visit to her apartment at the beginning of the week. In the time since, he had sweat through restless nights while he'd pictured her lying next to him, and beneath him, and on top of him.

Though their moments together had never lacked passion, he couldn't stand to touch her again until they were completely naked and in a bed. Sex on the kitchen counter had a lot going for it, but it couldn't be prolonged, what with the balancing of limbs and the sharp edges and all. He wanted her outstretched next to him, where they could move slowly and gently, or fast and hard. Preferably both. All night long.

And then he wanted to hand her a hundred thousand dollars and send her on her merry way.

He swept a hand through his hair, laughing at his own absurdity. Jacey deserved better, and that's what she would get once she had enough money to leave town, or go to school, or whatever she had planned. He was pretty sure she didn't intend to stay in that dingy apartment forever. After she was gone, he would just have to find something else to focus on.

Which shouldn't be too hard, considering when Insomnia crowned Jacey the winner of the contest, he would be the company's lead man. No more pretending to revere his father, no more struggling to get his designs and ideas into production.

He wound his way through the crowd of women. Time to put the plan into action. On top of keeping his hormones in check, he had to find an opportune moment to swap out some of the voters' ballots with his own to ensure Jacey advanced to the second round. And he had to do it without his assistant noticing, which wouldn't be easy since she was running the show and nothing seemed to escape her watchful eye.

"No, no, absolutely not," Kim barked into her cell phone. She handed one of the contestants an earring and shook her head at another girl who was wearing one shoe.

"Can't you ladies keep track of your own stuff? How badly do you want this?" She turned back to the phone. "No, I was talking to someone else. Listen, just get me the paperwork and—fine. Great. Gotta run."

She disconnected the call and released a huge sigh.

"Need some help?" Alex offered. Maybe if he stayed busy, his mind would quit wandering to the dressing room where Jacey was changing clothes. He had too much to accomplish tonight to let himself get so easily distracted.

Kim shoved a loose lock of hair back into her ponytail and dabbed at her face with a tissue. "God, it's hot in here. Yes, I need help. If you would, please go find out what's taking those last few girls so long to get dressed. We're getting ready to start."

Great. He'd been trying to keep his mind off the dressing room, and now he was headed straight for it.

Well, he had asked. "Sure. See you when the show starts."

"Uh-huh."

Alex watched her retreating back. Was the show was the only thing on her mind? In all their years of working together, she had never held a conversation with him that was strictly business. Maybe she had finally gotten over the mistake of a night they'd spent together. What a refreshing change that would be.

He turned and made his way to the dressing room door. Giggles and concerned squeals about makeup sounded from the other side.

He cleared his throat and knocked. "Um, ladies? You about ready to go in there?"

The door burst open, and a pretty young brunette appeared, her hair piled on her head in a jumble of curls. The pale blue of her gown matched her eyes, and for a brief moment, Alex worried he'd been too quick to assume Jacey would be the only one to enchant the audience with her beauty. Though he believed she was by far the most beautiful woman in the competition, the other girls had plenty to offer in terms of enticing customers—and votes.

Damn his father. Fixing this contest would cause Insomnia more harm than good if the potential patrons who filled the auditorium ended up in an uproar over the winner.

"We're ready!" answered a chorus of soprano voices. The brown-haired girl winked at him, then she and the rest of the women filed past him and headed backstage.

Wait a minute. Where was Jacey? Sure that he'd seen all the other contestants leave, he walked into the dressing room and closed the door behind him.

82

"Jacey?"

No answer. He peered into the shower area, walked past a dozen lighted mirrors and bits of makeup scattered on the counters, but the place was empty of people.

How would Jacey make it to the second round if she didn't show up to begin with? He reached into his pocket and wrapped his fingers around his phone before remembering he couldn't call her. If he forgave her for this, he was going to buy her a damn phone.

"I'm here."

He turned, relieved to hear the sound of her voice. She stood in a corner, clad in the white bathrobe Insomnia had provided for all the contestants. He wanted to ask her why she wasn't dressed, but something in her eyes said now wasn't the time for a lecture. At least her hair and makeup were done.

"I'm glad," he said, then noticed the anguish in her expression. He took her by the arm and led her to a chair, then pulled up one for himself and sat down beside her.

"What's wrong?"

"Nothing. I'm running a little behind."

"Bull. You look depressed as hell. What's going on?"

Silence. She stared into her lap and blew out a breath heavy with torment. "I got fired."

"What?"

"A couple of days ago. My supervisor fired me."

"Any particular reason?"

"I slapped a customer." She said it like she was telling him what she had for breakfast that morning.

He stared at her, trying to imagine those dainty hands inflicting pain on someone. "You hit a customer? What happened?"

"He grabbed my ass and asked me to try on a bra for him."

That son of a bitch. Alex's blood pressure rose. Her hands might be dainty, but Jacey was strong. Thank God. He was so proud of her, yet so overwhelmed by a fierce need to pummel this guy. "Please tell me that's not true. And why was this your fault and not his?"

"Oh, it was his fault. But the manager walked in just in time to see me hit him, and the guy played it like I was overreacting to an innocent question about the merchandise."

She moved her stare to the ceiling and dampness formed in the corners of her eyes. He wanted to hold her, but he didn't think she would want a man's touch at that moment.

"Jacey, that's bullshit. Tell me your supervisor's name. I can—"

"No."

"There are security cameras in every store. We'll be able to prove the guy was coming on to you and you'll get your job back. I'll see to it personally that this half-witted manager loses his job instead."

"Not necessary. The last thing I need is him stalking me because he's pissed off about being fired. I'll find another job."

"Where?"

"I don't know, but it won't be difficult. Most of the managers around here are more concerned with tits and ass than they are with qualifications."

She held her robe against her chest, her arms wrapped protectively around her. There was no mistaking the defeat in her posture. In that condition, there was no way she could take the stage with the confidence and sensuality the competition required.

He didn't know what to say and he felt like a fool. She looked pained at the thought of being a sex object for another minute, and that was exactly what he was asking her to do—in fact, it was what he was setting her up to do—in the competition.

He envisioned her dangerous neighborhood, and now, her lack of a paycheck. A crazy idea occurred to him, one he was certain she'd shoot down in a heartbeat, but he had to try. He needed to make up for the angst his company had caused her— and protect her from hurting anymore.

"Move in with me," he blurted. "I mean, temporarily. Just until the contest is over. You won't have much time to look for a job while you're preparing for the next two shows."

She looked surprised, but she didn't bite his head off. She just smiled and said, "What makes you so sure I'll be around for the next two shows?"

Oops.

He hooked his finger under her chin. "Because you look amazing and you're about to blow five thousand people away. I know you can do this."

Her lips curved slowly upward until that beautiful smile erased her gloom. Alex brushed the backs of his fingers over her neck. He wanted to touch her, but it was way too late to redo her face and hair, which he would definitely mess up. Jacey shivered, reached up and covered his hand with hers.

She brought his hand down and squeezed it. "That's nice of you, but I paid enough rent to get me through a few more days. After that, I'll find a way to get by. I always do."

Alex nodded, not at all surprised by her answer. If she wanted to be on her own, he had to respect that. Plus, if everything went according to plan, she'd have the hundred thousand in hand in two weeks...still, she'd be homeless for a week while he sat alone in his big, empty condo. How senseless was that?

It's not your choice. He bit his tongue to keep from asking her again.

"I guess I'm ready, then." Jacey looked down at herself and put her hands on her knees. "My outfit's underneath."

"Can I see?" He trailed a teasing finger down the center of her robe.

She gave him a look of warning and swatted his hand away. "No peeking. I want to hear your reaction after you see the show."

"Go get 'em," he whispered, and kissed her lightly on the ear. "Just think about how it felt when I touched you the other night."

"I look forward to not being interrupted by your pager." With a seductive wink, she sauntered off.

Alex grinned, but he couldn't shake his concern. There was more to Jacey Cass than he could imagine, and the contest was only making her plight worse.

He sighed and took his seat in the front of the auditorium, beginning to regret he had ever dreamed up this competition.

But his regret changed to satisfaction after the curtain opened. The first contestant pranced out to center stage in a hot pink jacquard bustier. Her thick black hair bouncing around her breasts, she turned her back to the crowd and shimmied to seductive music, her small, tight ass peeking out from beneath the fabric.

Scores of people cheered. The girl spun around and waved, then blew a kiss to the crowd as she made her exit. Alex clapped along with everyone else, approving of the whistles and shouts of excitement the performance had garnered. At this rate, the competition would be a huge success.

Alex Vaughn, CEO had a catchy ring to it. In a couple of weeks, the title would belong to him.

By random selection, Jacey was the twenty-second model to take a turn on stage. As the night went on and the women continued to deliver stellar performances, Alex hoped being on the last leg of the show would work in Jacey's favor since the audience would more clearly remember the last few appearances of the evening. But when she stepped out from behind the curtain, he knew that regardless of her place in the pecking order, she was a sight the crowd wouldn't soon forget.

At first glance, he saw only a white robe similar to the one she'd worn in the dressing room, but made of silk. Then it dropped to the floor, unveiling a white gown with beaded straps. The material reached her knees but was sheer enough to reveal the lace bra and panties underneath. Alex was sure if he were a little closer to her, he'd be able to see what was beneath *that*.

His heart skipped a beat. While the man in him fully appreciated the erotic yet virginal vision that Jacey's clothing created, the professional in him couldn't help wondering if the risk she had taken would harm her. None of the other girls had chosen white—it sold well during wedding season but was much less popular this late in the year--nor had they worn anything that didn't cover what needed to be covered. Even the girl in hot pink had put some solid panties on before she'd shaken her booty for every news channel in Miami.

The contest's design called for the level of sensuality to rise with each show, culminating in the R-rated sexy finale. But Jacey had started so hot, Alex wondered what she'd do next time. He prayed for a positive reaction from the audience.

She approached a lavishly decorated bed in the middle of the stage, and the approving roar of the crowd drowned out his fears. Though the silhouette of her body was visible to everyone in the room due to strategic lighting, there was nothing risqué about her act. She lounged on the bed with her silver high heels crossed, her curly hair draped over one shoulder, and her mesmerizing blue eyes gazing out into the crowd. She looked like every man's wedding night fantasy.

Alex could barely breathe. Tonight, he vowed, she would be his reality.

Chapter Seven

Jacey was horny.

She was panicking too, while she stood behind Alex on his front stoop and listened to his keys jangle in the doorknob. *Two weeks*, she kept repeating to herself. Two weeks, and that was it.

The contest ended in exactly two weeks, the same day she had decided her living arrangement with him would cease. With any luck, she would be thousands of dollars richer. But even if she lost, she'd clean tables at the nearest fast-food heap before she would depend on Alex to keep a roof over her head for any longer than that. After spending the entire evening backstage considering his offer, she had finally agreed to stay with him so she could focus on the competition without stressing over finding a job. He was not her meal ticket. He was a generous friend and nothing more.

But they could still have really good sex.

At least, she hoped so, because half an hour ago someone had called Alex with the list of contestants advancing to the second round, and her name was on it. She'd yelped with joy when he told her. There had been so many gorgeous women, but she had made it. No doubt Alex's backstage pep talk had helped her performance, and she intended to thank him—thoroughly.

Her spirits dampened slightly when she stepped inside his condo. One look at his luxurious bachelor pad reminded her of the painful reason she'd chosen to remain anonymous at all those parties even while she allowed him inside her body. Her simple existence couldn't add anything of value to his pampered lifestyle, and she would never settle for being his spoiled, fruitless arm candy.

"Do you think you'll be comfortable here?" he asked.

He didn't sound snide or boastful, so she resisted the urge to snap at the ridiculous question. But he had seen her apartment—anything would be more comfortable than that.

"A million-dollar condo will probably suffice."

Alex let the comment slide. A flick of the light switch revealed a huge open room with hardwood floors, a flat TV hanging from the ceiling, and more of those framed paintings she didn't recognize but assumed cost more money than she made in a year. An entire wall of windows offered a breathtaking view of downtown Miami and the ocean beyond. She watched the city lights twinkle, eager to see what it would look like when the sun came up.

After placing her bags inside the front door, Alex took her hand and led her to a plush leather sofa. His touch, like always, made her forget—or at least ignore—that she felt like a bag lady in the face of such luxury.

Without a doubt, her mother's life would be different if she had lived in a place like this. Jacey squeezed Alex's hand, savoring the warmth of his fingers. It would feel so good if he traced a slow path from the crown of her hair to her neck, across her breasts and stomach and all the way down her legs...so nice if she drowned her troubles in their physical connection the way she had so many times before.

He watched her fingers caress his, and his gaze burned into her with an intensity she hadn't seen since the last party. She wet her lips. If he wanted her as much as she wanted him right now, her first night at his place would be anything but awkward.

She opened her mouth to ask him, but he spoke first. "Do you remember the night we met?"

Her vocal cords refused to work under the heat of his stare, so she just nodded.

"Can you still feel the first time I put my hands on your breasts, and my face between your legs?"

A jolt of electricity shot through her, originating in the spot on her neck where he gently sucked. Though three years had passed since their first meeting, she would *never* forget the long moments they'd spent in that deserted hotel bathroom. Her back pressed against the mirror, her skirt pushed up to her waist, and Alex dropping hot, wet kisses on her hips, her navel and lower.

She shivered. He looked up at her, and either his charming grin or his sexy bedroom eyes initiated her loss of control. She pulled him to her and kissed him hard, her lips joined to his and her tongue searching his mouth for the passion she didn't know how she'd always survived an entire year without.

His hands roamed her back, moving over the fabric of her shirt and making their way beneath it. Her skin tingled wherever he touched.

"That night was...nice," she whispered, her breath shaking.

He trailed his lips along her ear. "It was amazing."

A moment later he lay above her on the couch. He kissed her collarbone, brushing his palms over her curves. She hurt for him, wanted to tear her clothes off and fill her body with him. He lifted her shirt and took her nipple into his mouth, then dipped his thumb into her navel and danced his fingertips along the edge of her jeans. Her hips reached for his touch.

"Can people see us?" she asked when she spotted the massive uncovered windows beside them.

"I doubt it, we're too high. Would it bother you if they could?"

"Not at all."

She grabbed his neck and kissed him again, more turned on than she had ever been in her life. But as he moved to undress her and the erotic fantasy began to turn into another quickie, she forced herself to put a few inches of distance between them.

"Alex..."

"Yes, baby?"

"I want to take our time tonight."

He looked at her, a smile forming on his sexy mouth. "I do owe you for last time, don't I?"

"You don't owe me anything. I just want to be with you."

She almost clapped a hand over her mouth when she heard the words out loud. That statement had so many implications, and she didn't want him to think she was desperate. But what would explain the driving need to feel her naked body entwined with his for hours on end? She craved him.

She craved his *body*. Yeah, that's what she meant.

Alex brushed his thumb over her lips. "I can give you all night, if you think that's enough."

"It'll be a good start. Let me go—what do the sophisticated women say? Freshen up?"

He chuckled and pointed down the hall. "First door on the left."

Moments later, she stood in front of the mirror and surveyed his posh bathroom. It boasted black marble countertops, a double vanity with faucets so shiny she was sure he didn't clean them himself, and a huge whirlpool tub in one corner that commanded attention. Plush navy accent rugs and matching towels gave the room a masculine, homey feeling. It was a far cry from the cramped little cell she used at home.

She looked beyond her reflection and saw Alex in the doorway, watching her. Time to turn on the charm. There was one thing she wanted tonight, and she'd come into this bathroom to make sure it happened.

"I just had to look at it one more time," she said, fingering the thin white fabric she'd changed into. The perks of being a semi-finalist included getting to keep the winning lingerie. "It's so beautiful."

He stepped up behind her and put his hands on her shoulders, and the heat in his touch sent a shiver pulsing through her.

"I think the model makes it look that way."

Jacey turned and tugged playfully at the dress shirt, still neatly tucked into his pants, that he'd worn for the show earlier that evening. "You're flattering me."

"Maybe."

"You're not going to sleep in this, are you?"

He pinned her with an impassioned look. "I hope not."

With a demure smile tossed in his direction, she strolled past him and into his connecting bedroom. Her insides twisted into an anticipatory knot. He wanted her.

"I'm sorry." Her gaze flickered between Alex and his big, cushy bed. "I shouldn't be so presumptuous. Do you want me to sleep on the couch?"

He shook his head, his wanton stare still trained on her. "Don't be ridiculous. You can have the bed as long as you're staying here."

"Thanks."

She flashed him another smile and returned to the bathroom, where he stood in the same spot in front of the mirror. He was trying hard to go along with her game, but she couldn't wait any longer.

She pulled the clip from her hair and let the curls tumble down her back, shaking her head a bit and using her fingers to tame unruly strands.

"Oh, that feels better," she said with a drawn-out little moan.

Alex reached out and took her by the arms. "You're driving me crazy."

"Me? Do you want me to go?"

"You know that's not what I mean."

She locked her eyes with his and gave him her very best *do me* stare. "What do you mean, then?"

He seized her waist and pulled her up to sit on the countertop, just as he had done in her kitchen. She squealed when her bottom hit the cold marble surface, but Alex's kisses quickly warmed her.

"Remember having sex on the bathroom sink?" he asked.

The urgency in his touch drove her wild. "I'd sure love to."

"Let me give you a recap."

He pushed the straps from her shoulders. The gown pooled around her waist and he wasted no time discarding the lacy bra, leaving her bared to his gaze. Her nipples stood at attention and he closed his lips over one of them.

She rested her head against the mirror, gasping with pleasure, losing herself in the simultaneous movements of his mouth on her breasts and his hands on her thighs. She fumbled with the buttons of his shirt until it fell open and she could run her fingers through the dark hair on his chest. Their lips met again, and she grabbed his back in a frenzy of need. She wiggled out of the nightie and he tossed it aside, but she jumped down from the counter before he could go down on her.

"Where are you going?" he objected.

She pressed her palms against his chest and kissed him. "It's your turn."

Eager to taste him, she sank to her knees, drawing her hands down his body until she came to rest on the bath mat. She loosened his belt buckle, and when his pants and boxers were on the floor next to her, she wrapped her hands around his legs and stroked the head of his cock with her tongue.

He groaned. She took him into her mouth and laved his shaft, moving one hand to his balls and the other behind him, where she scraped her nails lightly over his smooth ass. She sucked him hard, the way she knew he liked it, even though she wanted to smile at the intense pleasure she was obviously giving him.

His noises grew louder, and she tasted a drop of moisture that signaled he was getting close. With one more teasing suck, she stood up and took her place on top of the counter, opening her legs and inviting him to enjoy something better than her mouth. He placed his hands on either of her knees and pressed his length all the way inside her.

"Does that feel all right?"

She dropped her forehead onto his shoulder. "It feels incredible."

She sat on the edge of the counter, clutching his strong arms and feeling his muscles contract with each thrust. How in the world had once a year ever been enough for her?

"Here, baby, turn around," he said, and she slid down from the sink.

Yeah, she remembered this too. Filled with anticipation once more, she turned and watched in the mirror as he pushed into her again. He moved with more force this time, and she moaned while he stroked and pleasured something deep inside her.

Years ago in the hotel bathroom, it had ended this way. Thrilling as that had been at the time, Jacey was far too hot and bothered to stop now.

"Alex," she breathed. He lowered his face to hers and nibbled at her earlobe. "Take me to your bed."

Suddenly, she was overwhelmed by the kindness he had shown her over the past few weeks. He'd driven all the way to her apartment because she didn't have a phone, encouraged her backstage when she'd hit rock bottom, offered her a place to stay...and he had seemed genuinely thrilled for her when she had gotten word that evening that she'd advanced to the semi-finals—like he truly wanted to see her succeed in the future.

It was strange, but now that she knew he cared about more than her body, all she wanted was to go to bed with him.

He took her hand and led her to his bedroom, where she nestled into the most comfortable sheets she'd ever touched. He knelt above her, and she held him close while he slipped slowly into her body. She kissed his neck, releasing a sound of abandon when he reached up and took two fistfuls of her hair, gently tugging at it while they made love.

She didn't know how much time had passed when they shared their last release, her body too exhausted to consider going for it again. The evening's flurry of activity finally caught up with her and she began to fall asleep, safe and comfortable in his arms. She kissed him one more time, and his warm, moist body relaxed against her.

Yet while she drifted off, that two-week deadline nagged her. She had so much to accomplish in so little time—like winning the competition and getting out of Alex's life before it hurt her to leave.

Chapter Eight

Alex peeked into his bedroom and smiled at the mess of blonde hair piled near his headboard. Jacey lay on her stomach, the blankets pulled up to her neck and her face buried in the pillow.

He suppressed a chuckle, then walked to the kitchen and set a bag of bagels and assorted spreads from his favorite deli on the table. He whistled while he brewed a pot of coffee, unable to quell the feeling of being light on his feet last night's lovemaking had instilled in him, despite the guilt that tugged at the back of his mind.

She would never have to know he'd fixed the contest. Her chances of winning were high anyway, and practically everyone in Miami knew he was about to take his father's place as CEO. When both happened at the same time, it wouldn't seem odd to Jacey or anyone else.

So why did he feel like a villain covering up a crime?

He heard the shower turn on, so he sat down to look through the mail he'd picked up on his way back from getting breakfast. Bills, a couple of business magazines, a letter from his mother...and a manila envelope addressed in handwriting he didn't recognize. A staff member had probably forwarded some designer's résumé for him to review.

A frustrated groan rumbled in his throat while he stuck his finger under the flap to open it, trying to figure out how he could scrap Insomnia's plan to interview outside candidates. He had been working on a lingerie collection for years, whenever he found a spare moment. But as usual, his father had nixed the idea of putting Alex's name on what was sure to be the company's biggest hit—the collection that the Sleepless Siren winner would debut. Fortunately, he would soon have his father's power to insist on having things a certain way, and he'd use that to his advantage if they didn't find a designer nothing short of genius by the time he got promoted.

A black-and-white picture fell out of the envelope, and he almost spit his coffee all over it.

Clear as day, the photographer had captured an image of him and Jacey kissing in front of her kitchen window. The blinds had been wide open, but they'd been too occupied to notice. A note scrawled on the side margin warned: *Stay away from her, or this is the cover of next week's Daily Sun.*

"What are you doing?" demanded a voice behind him. Jacey's hand lashed out and snatched the paper. "What is this?"

"Someone's hobby." He shook his head and let her have the photo. No point in hiding the problem since she already knew something was up.

She took it and sat next to him at the table. With damp hair and a face washed clean of makeup, she looked less like the vixen he'd always known and more like the pretty young woman that she was—at least, until her face turned beet red with anger.

"Who would do something like this?"

"No idea." He shrugged. "You got any bitter ex-boyfriends?"

"Of course not. I haven't had a boyfriend since high school."

"What?"

She blushed even darker. "I mean, I've dated casually since then, of course. I just haven't been in a relationship."

Alex nodded, wanting to ask her why but deciding it wasn't his business. Last night had been incredible, but it hadn't changed anything. She was only staying with him until the end of the competition, and he wouldn't have any time to invest in a serious relationship while he was running Insomnia. Besides, they both had more important problems to deal with at the moment—like the stalker threatening to take their affair public.

He could imagine the headline. *Insomnia CEO-in-training reaps benefits of modeling competition.*

Ouch.

This story could not go beyond the envelope he'd taken it from. The company would be forced to drop Jacey from the contest to avoid a huge scandal. And if that alone didn't ruin his career due to his father's ridiculous ultimatum, word around town that he had taken advantage of a contestant— whether it was true or not—would damage his reputation beyond repair.

What was he going to do? He couldn't risk Jacey's place in the competition, but he certainly couldn't put her out on the street without a dime to her name. Besides, their sexual encounters seemed to distract her from her problems, and her confidence was a critical part of her ability to perform on stage. Last night in bed, there had been no doubt she was the same woman who tantalized him each year at the company party. If she could get the audience to feel *that* sexy by the final round, she wouldn't even need his help to win.

On top of the whole mess, he didn't particularly want to stay away from her, anyway. He'd felt that way long before he'd been threatened by the head case who took the photo.

He rubbed his face, searching his brain for a way to end this media frenzy before it started. Still looking uncomfortable at the discussion of her past, Jacey picked through his mail while she sipped a glass of orange juice.

"Melanie Vaughn?" she inquired.

"My mom."

"Ah." With a nod, she put the unopened letter back on the table and began to spread strawberry cream cheese on a bagel. "You guys close?"

Alex hesitated, not sure this conversation was any lighter than that of Jacey's past relationships. "Yeah. The divorce was pretty hard on her."

"Oh, I'm sorry. She left when you were a kid?"

"No, my parents divorced just a couple of years ago, actually."

She looked up at that. "Really?"

"I'm surprised you didn't read about it. The media had a heyday with it."

"I don't make a habit of reading that garbage." She thought for a moment, then made a noise of disbelief. "Wow. And here I thought the almighty Vaughns didn't know pain."

His coffee went down the wrong pipe.

He coughed. "Yeah. Right. We're immune."

"Well, you've got one hell of a protective layer. It's called money."

"People with money don't feel pain?"

"Not as much pain as people without money feel."

His mind swam with memories of his parents' frosty marriage, his disappointment at never having siblings, and the years of Thanksgivings and Christmases spent alone, usually in his office. "That's completely untrue."

"Baloney. If my mother had money, she'd be...something. She wouldn't be sprawled on the bed in her trailer with crack in one hand and some guy's dick in the other. If she had even a tiny fraction of the money you have, maybe she'd actually have bought condoms and I wouldn't even exist."

She stared into her lap. Alex watched her for a moment, digesting her words. His gut clenched when he imagined the hardships she must have been through as a child. No wonder she never liked to talk about her past. It sounded even lonelier than his, and definitely more difficult.

He reached across the table and took her hand. "Then I'm glad she doesn't have money."

She gave him a little smile. "You're flattering me again."

"It's not hard to do."

After a moment of silent thought, Jacey continued eating. He couldn't stop watching her. Curiosity about her life overcame him, and he waited until she had finished before questioning her.

"If you don't mind me asking, do you know your father?"

She froze.

"You do mind me asking."

"No." With a shake of her head, she placed her knife and napkin on top of her empty plate and dropped her hands into her lap. "I don't care. It's just that I haven't talked to anybody about my parents before."

"Well, you don't have to talk about it." He sipped his coffee and tried to look casual. "I was just curious."

"I didn't know him. I doubt my mom even knew him, aside from the two seconds they were doing...what they were doing."

She paused, but he didn't press for more information. He had a feeling the memories she dredged up wouldn't be pleasant, and he didn't want her to revisit any of that unless she wanted to tell him about it.

"My mother had issues. We were dirt poor and she offered sex to every man alive to get money for drugs and food. There was a different guy in the house every day. Instead of doing something to solve our problems, she got high and forgot about them. She took every form of aid imaginable—welfare, shelters, money from anyone who would spare it. When I was fourteen, she asked me to prostitute myself too. One big happy whore family."

She took a breath. "I don't want to be anything like her. So you see why I couldn't take your offer for the modeling job, and I can't take financial aid to go to college. I need to do this on my own."

Alex expected she might cry, but she looked at him with conviction. He was so proud of her. She could have easily ended up like her mother.

He took her hand, but his growing feelings for her disturbed him. How would he let her go, especially now that he knew what a hellish life she'd been forced to live? How could he send her back to that when all he wanted to do was protect her, keep her safe in his condo, and have the opportunity to talk to her and touch her every night instead of once a year?

On second thought, she didn't work for Insomnia anymore. They wouldn't even have the annual parties to look forward to. Suddenly, the future he was risking his reputation to make happen looked lonely and bleak.

When she'd agreed to move in with Alex, Jacey had told him to screw himself if he expected her to clean house and do his laundry. She had every intention of paying him two weeks' worth of expenses once she had the money, but acting as his personal assistant when she was sleeping with him every night would feel eerily similar to trading sex for help with his errands.

Yet the urge to get a closer look at his personal items had grown irresistible, and playing housemaid gave her a good excuse. Despite her initial refusal to do his chores, she now sat on the living room sofa with her hands in a basket full of clean, soft, masculine clothes. They were still warm from the dryer, and she held one of his T-shirts to her cheek, inhaling the scent of the detergent.

It was Monday, so Alex had gone to work and she had his castle to herself. Across the room, sun glinted off the pure blue ocean and streamed through the wall of glass. She eyed the shiny floors and the spacious kitchen stocked with goodies. After staying in a place like this, the notion of calling her piece of crap apartment *home* made her sick to her stomach.

And why? It had been fine before. It had been more than fine until she'd made the idiotic decision of being with Alex for more than a one-night stand, and now his swank lifestyle had poisoned her thoughts, made her materialistic and wishy-washy, someone who dreamed of living the good life instead of working hard toward supporting herself.

She'd gone and done the one thing she had sworn never to do. She had let herself depend on a man to give her things she couldn't afford on her own—and she was sleeping with him in return.

She had become her mother.

With a noise of disgust, she tossed Alex's shirt back into the basket. Instead of folding and putting them away like she'd planned, she dumped the pile of rumpled clothes onto his bed.

She grabbed a couple of twenties off the stack of bills he had left on the kitchen counter, realizing she couldn't go anywhere without a cab because on top of everything else, her car had stopped running and was currently lifeless outside her apartment building. Once again, she tried to ignore how much she loathed depending on his money. Whether he liked it or not, she'd pay him back. Soon.

When she walked into Monica's shop, she spotted her friend in a corner of the store, adjusting a slinky ivory slip she'd draped over a mannequin.

"Wow, that's gorgeous. Is it new?"

Monica looked over and smiled. "Yup. I plan on putting it up front in a month or so, when people start their holiday shopping. What do you think?"

Jacey circled the plastic torso, admiring the slip's waist-hugging pleats and the two ruffled strips of material at the very short hem. "Incredibly sexy. Beautiful. I've never seen anything like it, not even at—"

A light bulb clicked on in her head. "Insomnia," she finished. "Do you think I could use that for the contest?"

"You don't have to wear their stuff?"

"Not necessarily."

To be honest, she wasn't sure about the rules on that, but she figured it wouldn't hurt to run her idea by Alex. He had a lot of pull in that company.

"They would announce your name and everything. It could be great publicity for you."

Monica left the mannequin and patted Jacey's hand. "Of course, honey. You're welcome to it. I've got one in the back that should be just your size."

"Great. Thank you so much."

"Now what brings you here? You don't have a job yet? You know, my door is always—"

"No, absolutely not." Jacey waved off the suggestion as they made their way to the front of the store. "You've done enough for me. Actually, I'm staying with Alex—*only* until the contest is over and I can find another job," she added when her friend's eyebrows lifted in surprise.

"Wow. That's pretty generous of him."

"Yeah. He's not such a bad guy."

Monica laughed. "Do I need to say I told you so?"

"Please don't." Jacey fingered a beaded purse on display at the end of the sales desk. "I just came to talk because I need a break from being a helpless moocher. What's been going on around here?"

"Nothing much with me. Oh, but Danielle got an interview at Insomnia! I can't believe I forgot to tell you."

"Really? That's fantastic."

"Yeah, she didn't make the competition but apparently somebody liked her audition, because she's got an appointment with William Vaughn himself."

"You're kidding. That's great news. Wish her luck for me."

Pride and happiness filled Jacey's chest. It thrilled her to see these two women, who'd started out not much better off than Jacey and her own mother, had risen to the challenge and now enjoyed the kind of success most people only dreamed about. Though it hurt that her mother hadn't bothered to work toward securing their future, she was incredibly grateful to be a part of Monica and Danielle's life. Where would she be without the kindness they had shown her ten years ago?

Probably streetwalking and trying to take care of her fatherless children. She shivered.

Her gaze fell on the slip again. After all this time, she had a chance to do something special for Monica. Her business would double if people heard the shop's name announced during the competition.

She couldn't let Alex coddle her any longer. Not when her friends were solid proof that a rough start didn't have to mean forever depending on someone else. She had plans for her future, and it was time to put them into action.

She tried on the size Monica had in stock, and upon discovering that it fit, put it in a bag along with some gorgeous matching sandals and hopped back into her waiting cab.

Her mood soured the instant she walked into Alex's office. The rude brown-haired woman sat at the desk outside his door, and Jacey cursed herself for failing to pay her phone bill. If she had her cell, she could have called and asked him to meet her outside. But it had been a choice between phone and water, and she didn't want to give up showers if she could help it.

She cleared her throat, and Kim looked up in surprise.

"I need to see Alex, please," Jacey said with false brightness.

Kim didn't look convinced. She dropped the papers she had been studying. "I'm sorry, he's busy."

"With what?"

"Work!" she shouted, then quickly lowered her voice. "What are you doing here? This is a place of business. You can have your playtime somewhere else."

Jacey held up the bag, gritting her teeth. "This *is* business. I need to see him."

She crossed to Alex's door and knocked hard.

Kim jumped up from her chair. "I don't know who you think you are, but—"

The door opened. Alex's eyes bounced back and forth like he was watching a Wimbledon match. "Ladies, is there a problem out here? Why are we yelling in the middle of the office?" His irritated gaze landed on Kim.

Jacey bit back a smile. Alex was this woman's supervisor, and he sounded sexy when he got bossy.

"Hi, honey," she said sweetly. "I need to have a quick meeting with you, if that's okay."

Kim's eyes bulged.

Alex coughed and took Jacey's arm. "All right, but make it quick."

He hustled her into his office but dropped his professional demeanor when the door closed. "Are you trying to get me in trouble?"

He slipped his arms around her waist and drew her close to him. She smiled, adoring how handsome and successful he looked in his crisp white shirt and dark tie.

"Why do you say that?"

"You just called me *honey* in front of my assistant."

"I was just trying to piss her off. We don't get along very well."

"So I've noticed."

She put her hands in his hair and drew his mouth close to hers. "You look hot."

"I could say the same about you."

"Then kiss me."

He did, and the bag dropped from her grip, the clothing forgotten as she lost herself in the heat of their kiss and the feel of his hands on her jeans.

"Damn, I'd like to get these off you."

"I'd like you to do me right on top of your desk."

Alex grunted, kissing her and trying to tug her pants down at the same time. Jacey laughed and kicked her shoes off, then pulled off her jeans and panties while Alex opened his belt and yanked down his zipper.

Her exposed flesh tingled with need. He crushed her to his chest and thrust his tongue between her lips. She perched on the surface of his desk with her legs wide. When she caught sight of his thick erection she pushed her hips forward, begging him to enter her.

He stood between her knees and feverishly kissed her neck while he pushed inside her. She braced her hands on the desk and looked to the ceiling, forcing back her cries so his colleagues wouldn't hear her and figure out what was going on in his office. His movements were hard and rough, giving both of them the intense satisfaction they craved.

Despite her efforts to stay silent, a moan escaped when she came. Alex followed with his own climax, then dropped his head to her shoulder and released a slow breath.

She slid down from the desk and they both dressed, exchanging mischievous glances as they did so.

"So," Alex said, somewhat breathlessly, "is that why you needed to see me?"

She spotted the bag on the floor and snatched it up, her face warm. She'd come here to do Monica a favor, not to get laid. Could she be any more selfish?

"Actually, no. I came to talk to you about a design for the contest. My friend Monica is a fantastic designer. I was thinking I could wear this for Saturday's show, and if it's a hit, you guys could do some business together. She's amazing."

She took the garment from the bag and presented it to him with gusto. He just blinked.

"So?" she prodded when he didn't answer. What was the matter with him? Was he blind? "What do you think?"

"Um, I...it's beautiful. Honestly. But Insomnia doesn't really need another designer right now."

So he wasn't blind, but he *was* lying to her. Insomnia had advertised its designer search right along with the Sleepless Siren contest. Supposedly the two events would culminate in the unveiling of the company's most amazing collection ever, or something to that effect.

"Well, okay," she said, deciding not to push the issue. "But I could still wear this in the contest, right? I mean, that would be enough publicity for her."

He rubbed his chin. "I don't know, Jacey. The contestants are supposed to wear items that are sold at Insomnia. Isn't there anything that interests you in the current collection? We've got some gorgeous—"

"No, no, I totally agree. Everything Insomnia sells is gorgeous. I was just thinking that if you were willing to work with her, this would be a good way to give the audience a preview of something new. I'm going last this time, and it would end the show with a bang, you know?"

"I...yeah." Alex sighed and shook his head. "I'm sorry, but I don't think that's possible. I'd have to pull a ton of strings, and there just isn't enough time."

Her heart sank. The detached tone of his voice made it clear he wasn't being straight with her. Since when couldn't he tell her the truth? And after the way she'd made love with him last night, and a few minutes ago.

A knot lodged in her throat. For the first time, she questioned her trust in him, and her doubts ripped a chasm in the closeness they had so recently shared. What was with the business talk about pulling strings? Why couldn't he do her this one favor simply because it meant so much to her, and he cared for her?

He *did* care for her, didn't he?

"I didn't think it would be that big of a deal." Unreasonable anger welled inside her. "Considering the benefits you're getting at home every night. And in your office."

His mouth opened and closed like a fish out of water. "Is that why you're sleeping with me? So I'll do you a favor?"

Jacey froze, her worst nightmare coming true right before her eyes. *Was* she exchanging sex for a chance at success? For the opportunity to give something back to Monica? Hadn't she just said as much to him?

The idea was so horrifying, she couldn't even answer. She turned and left the office, closing the door quietly behind her so Kim wouldn't suspect there was a problem. She hoped against hope that Alex was wrong.

She stared at the floor, so engrossed in her fears she almost crashed into a young woman coming out of Alex's father's corner office.

"Oh, excuse me."

The girl flashed her a big grin. "No problem."

She approached Kim's desk, and for a moment, Jacey watched with interest. Since Alex's parents were divorced, she supposed William Vaughn's personal life was his own business, but that woman looked even younger than her. Much younger.

Oh, well. The man was rich and powerful, and she'd seen the covers of enough Hollywood tabloids to know May-December romances were trendy. She headed for the exit. She'd left Monica's dress in Alex's office, but she wasn't about to go back and get it. He would see it and bring it home that evening.

"Thank you, Ms. Starr." Behind her, the girl chattered excitedly. "I can't wait to see my photos on Insomnia's website. I have to go home and tell my mom."

Jacey heard the rustling of paper, then Kim's voice. "Please sign this release form. Congratulations."

No way.

The girl had scored a modeling gig? She lived with her parents?

And she'd just come out of William's office with flushed cheeks and rumpled hair?

Jacey waited one more second, then shook her head, pushed open the double doors, and headed for the elevator.

Impossible.

Kim scanned the office for potential eavesdroppers before she snatched up her buzzing phone. "Thank you for calling Insomnia. This is Kim, how may I help you?"

"It's Robert."

She released an exasperated sigh at the sound of her private investigator's voice. This afternoon had brought several minutes of listening to Alex screw Blondie in his office, and she'd been *this* close to calling Robert herself and demanding answers.

"I thought it might be you. And it's about time. So what do you know?"

"I'm sorry, Ms. Starr, but they show no signs of breaking up. In fact, she appears to be living with him now."

"You're joking."

"I followed them to his residence several days ago, and since then, you can't find one without the other. They hardly come out at all as it is."

"Damn it!" Kim pounded the arm of her chair and lowered her voice. "What about the photos you took? Did he get them?"

"He got them, but they didn't have the desired effect. On the contrary, the whole thing seems to have drawn them closer together."

Fabulous. William still hadn't told her exactly why he wanted her to sabotage Jacey, but how in the world was she going to get the girl out of the contest when Alex played her bodyguard during every waking moment?

And possibly every night too. Kim shivered at the disgusting image of Alex in bed with that bimbo, but she was quickly consoled by thoughts of the nights she'd spent with William.

"Okay," she resigned. "Thanks, Robert. Just keep an eye on them and tell me if anything changes. I can see I'll have to step up my efforts."

"Yes, ma'am."

She hung up, licked the tip of her finger, and sifted through the files of the twenty remaining contestants. In a matter of seconds she found her—the beautiful brown-haired girl who looked like Katelyn. Amber Lynn Harris had come in second after the first round. Only Jacey had received more votes.

That was about to change, Kim would see to that. She grabbed the phone again and dialed Amber's number, and soon the young woman answered.

"Amber, this is Kim Starr, coordinator of Insomnia's Sleepless Siren contest. I noticed that you placed extremely high after the first round."

The girl squealed. "Really?"

"Really. Unfortunately, there's one contestant standing in your way and I'd like to offer you a deal. Do you want to win?"

There was a silence, and then Amber spoke in a cool, cunning voice. "Of course I want to win. What do you want?"

Kim almost laughed. A fellow schemer. At last, she had found someone who would help her make this happen.

"I want you to help me bring down Jacey Cass. With her out of the way, I can guarantee you the win. Are you willing to do that?"

"The blonde? Hell, yeah, what's the plan?"

They spoke for a few more minutes before Kim hung up with satisfaction. For Jacey to make the finals would take nothing less than a miracle.

Chapter Nine

Alex shut down his computer and gathered his things to leave, a difficult process with his fingers clenched the entire time.

Jacey would drive him mad, and not just because of his intense physical need for her. She was a fiery woman, and a scheming one at that. He didn't honestly believe she'd had sex with him in his office to butter him up before she presented her friend's design. Yet she did seem to expect that because they shared a bed, he should agree with her all the time. Why else would she have turned on him over something as simple as an outfit for the contest?

An uneasy tremor made its way through his stomach. He recalled the other women he had dated, and the way their angelic dispositions had turned sour after he'd made it clear he couldn't hand them a modeling contract. He could name half a dozen ex-girlfriends who had been in the relationship strictly for the benefits they'd hoped to receive while on the arm of Insomnia's heir.

It didn't make sense. Jacey had passed up every opportunity he had offered her with the company, and she hadn't left so much as her name after the first three years of getting naked with him at the annual party. Secrecy and isolation weren't exactly hallmarks of a person desperate to be famous.

No, she wasn't like the rest of them. She never had been.

Something had caused her mood to change in his office, though, and he wanted to know what it was. He planned to go home, sit her down and demand they stop playing games with each other—even if it meant that he had to come clean too. They could make their way through the Kama Sutra every night, but if they didn't trust each other, he might as well go back to his days of casual sex with any cute girl who wanted it.

That idea made for a huge turnoff when compared to making love with Jacey.

He stood to leave, and something on a chair across the room caught his eye—her dress. Guilt gnawed at him. He had never really looked at it, not closely enough to give it a fair chance.

The fabric grazed his fingers as he picked the dress up and placed it back on its hanger. It was soft. Luxurious. Definitely something he could imagine massaging against a woman's body before slipping it off. He inspected the garment's detail before placing it back in the bag, approving of the spaghetti straps and demi-cup bodice. Hot, hot, hot. It looked to be skintight aside from the ruffles at the bottom, which seemed to suggest a good girl being bad.

It would be stunning on Jacey.

Her friend was talented, no doubt. Alex probably could pull enough strings to get this costume into the competition, and only his desire to promote his own designs made him reject the idea. But even though he couldn't open Insomnia's doors to a new designer right away, Monica clearly knew what she was doing. He owed Jacey a huge apology for blowing off her request. He owed her something very special, and he could think of—

Wait. The doubts he'd nursed earlier still lingered in the back of his mind.

Talk first, sex later.

He released a breath, certain that would be easier said than done. He grabbed the garment bag and his briefcase, then headed out the door and drove too fast all the way home.

"Jacey!" he called when he walked inside. "Where are you? We need to talk."

She came out of his bedroom, a pile of towels in her arms. She looked wary, but no longer angry.

"What's up?"

He glanced at the towels. "What are you doing?"

"Finishing the laundry. I was bored this morning. Sorry if you can't find some of your clothes, I'm not sure I put them all in the right places."

Laundry? He closed his eyes and willed himself to focus on the things he wanted to talk about instead of the image she planted in his head. Standing there in a T-shirt and shorts with his laundry in her hands, she looked like she belonged there. Like she'd been there forever.

Like the wife he wanted to have someday, after Insomnia was his.

He cleared his throat and forced the vision out of his brain. He held up the bag. "We need to talk about this."

She brightened. "Did you change your mind?"

"I'm sorry, no. But I want to know why it's so important that you wear this."

"Because it's gorgeous and it would help me win."

"Is that all?"

"What other reason would there be?"

He crossed the room, took the towels from her, and set them on the sofa. Her eyes shifted in every direction, focused on everything in the place except him.

When he looked at her, the question he wanted to ask about her intentions stuck in his throat. He didn't want to hurt her, nor did he want to start a heavy conversation that would ruin their limited time together. He wanted to laugh with her, flirt with her, make love with her and forget everything else. Just like they had at the parties.

But that kind of freedom didn't exist outside of the no-strings affair they had shared until a few weeks ago. It was impossible to keep their relationship a casual one defined by sex when he cared so damn much about her.

The room had grown so silent he could hear the air flowing through his nostrils. Finally, he gathered his courage and held her gaze, hoping for the first time in his life that he was wrong.

"Jacey, is there something you want from me?"

One of her brows quirked up as though she thought he was referring to something in the bedroom. He rushed on before she could misunderstand him.

"Because if there is, I want you to tell me. I need you to. Please be honest with me. I won't be angry."

Her lips parted, confusion plastered across her lovely face. Alex longed to drop the issue and kiss her senseless instead.

"I'm not sure what you mean," she said. "What does this have to do with the dress or the contest?"

"I need to know if you're seeing me for any reason other than the fact that we have a good time together."

There. It was out.

She wasn't happy.

Her eyelids flew wide open and gave away her horror. She stepped away from him. "Jesus. You really do think I'm sleeping with you because I want something."

He dropped the bag at her feet and pointed at it. There wouldn't be any turning back now, so they might as well have it out.

"Why are you so bent on using this design? Why did you get so angry when I told you I couldn't do it?"

"Why are you asking me a million questions? I'm only staying here because you asked me to, remember? If I've worn out my welcome, I'll go."

Her fists clenched at her sides. She turned toward the door, and within half a second Alex planted himself in front of it.

"You don't have to go. Jacey, I'm sorry. You've in no way worn out your welcome. I just don't understand why you got so worked up in the office—"

"Because I'm trying to do something nice for my friend, okay? She saved my life. I owe her everything and I have nothing to give. I thought I'd make a bigger name for her if her shop was mentioned during the competition."

The fury in her eyes turned to desperation. Alex was ashamed for even considering the idea that she might be like the opportunistic women he'd known in the past.

He clutched her elbows, his voice low. "Why didn't you say so? You told me I should help you out because we're sleeping together."

"I was upset. I didn't mean it." The blue depths of her eyes locked onto him and she buried her hands in his hair. "Don't you know how you make me feel? Do you think I need any other reason to be with you?"

Her words poured into his veins, warming his body like brandy on a cold night. No other woman had ever said such a thing to him.

"My temper is short at times, I know," she said. "I just get scared sometimes that I won't make it."

Alex shut his eyes, pulling her closer to him. Her breath grazed his neck.

He was a fool. Jacey's young life had been filled with pain, yet here she was offering him sincere tenderness while he accused her of using *him*—the spoiled rich boy whose worst problems had involved too many women or not enough status.

Despite his father's wishes, he couldn't deceive her for another minute. He had the means to ease her pain and make her feel secure for once in her life. She wouldn't spend one more day being afraid, not if he could help it.

He took her face in his hands and smiled. "What would you say if I could guarantee you a source of income after the contest?"

"I've never come close to being guaranteed money, so I'd say you're crazy."

"You're going to win."

She gawked at him. "How do you know that?"

"Of all the contestants, my father picked you as the most beautiful and talented, and he wants you to win. I've agreed to arrange it. The money will be yours."

Silence. He watched her, barely able to contain his happiness at the joy this news would bring her. He waited for an excited squeal or an embrace filled with relief, but she just stared...and stared. Then, so quietly he almost didn't hear her, she spoke.

"God damn it, Alex."

Huh?

Maybe he hadn't explained everything. "I know you don't want to be a model, so I'll get you out of the contract. You can use the money for school or whatever you want."

A crazed look crossed her face. She looked down, then up, then directly at him. "Right. Great. You and your dad, saving the world one model at a time."

She turned, walked into his bedroom and closed the door.

Monica hugged Jacey before taking the bag from her and hanging the slip on a nearby garment rack. "I'm sorry, sweetheart. I know you would have looked fabulous wearing this."

Jacey shrugged, and a routine feeling of hopelessness settled within her. But this time, it wasn't about losing a chance at success. It was about losing a chance with Alex.

All this time she'd thought he was beginning to understand her and what she wanted out of life, but he had completely missed the ball. He had money and power, and he wanted to use it to provide her with a safety net in case she couldn't make it on her own.

She hated that. She wanted him to believe wholeheartedly that she *could* make it on her own.

If only she could make herself believe it too.

Monica glanced inside the empty bag, and Jacey realized she had forgotten half of the outfit. "Oh, crap. I left the shoes in Alex's office yesterday. He must not have seen them. I'm sorry, I'll go get them tonight."

"No problem."

The bell attached to the shop's door rang.

"Hey, honey," Monica greeted her daughter. "How was band practice?"

Danielle shrugged. "It was okay. One of the drum majors got a modeling job at Insomnia and it was all she could talk about."

The hollow sound of her voice caught Jacey's interest. Dani followed in her mother's fashionable footsteps and she'd always wanted to be a model. But when she mentioned Insomnia, her gaze fell straight to the floor.

Jacey pictured the young woman she'd run into outside of Alex's office. "Hey, does this girl happen to be tall with straight blonde hair?"

"No, she's a redhead. A senior. She was in the competition but got voted out after the first round, so they offered her some kind of deal for the new winter collection. Nothing huge if you ask me, not nearly enough for—whatever." Dani shot a worried look at her mother, then waved at Jacey and hurried to the back office.

Jacey gave Monica a curious look. "What was that about?"

Monica shook her head, wearing a disgusted expression. "I wanted to talk to you about that. Apparently this band girl was offered a modeling job last week in exchange for a favor."

"A favor?" The flushed face of the girl at Insomnia entered her mind once more. "Not *that* kind of favor."

"That's what she's telling everyone, though she could just be looking for attention. But Danielle swears it's true, that she's heard similar things from some of her friends."

Jacey's gut tied in knots. "Who exactly is requesting these 'favors'?"

"The man himself. William Vaughn."

She gasped. "No way."

"That's the word on the street."

"Does Alex know about this?" she asked out loud, even though Monica couldn't possibly know the answer.

"Don't know, hon. You're going to have to tackle that one yourself."

Jacey tried to wrap her mind around the absurd idea of William Vaughn sleeping with high school kids. She had noticed the models getting younger over the past couple of years, and Insomnia often held model search interviews at campuses across Miami to find new faces. But she'd always assumed they were trying to appeal to younger consumers.

A sickening thought occurred to her. "Danielle had an interview with William, didn't she? And she's beautiful. Tell me he never pulled that on her."

Monica's gaze darkened. "She'd never tell me if he did, but she came back from that interview looking more pissed off than I've ever seen her. I'm not convinced that nothing inappropriate took place, but I thank God she didn't take the job."

A foul-tasting lump formed in the back of Jacey's throat. She was thankful that unlike her own mother, Monica had kept her sexual escapades tucked away from her daughter's sight. Danielle was a smart girl with good morals, and at least if William or anyone else had made an offer, it sounded like she had done the right thing.

"I have to go," she said. "I'll bring your shoes back tomorrow, as soon as I can. I promise."

"No rush, honey," Monica replied as Jacey left the shop, but she was definitely in a rush. She had an overwhelming urge to sever any connection between Monica, Danielle and this possible corruption. The dress that had just yesterday been so important to her, she now wanted in no way used at Insomnia.

She had to get those shoes from Alex, and she was suddenly grateful he had turned down her idea to use Monica's design.

She tapped her foot in the back of the cab while it inched through rush hour traffic. Alex had expressed his fear that more photographers lurked and he didn't like that she wasn't hiding in the condo, but there was no way she could do that. Especially not now, when she had her own scandal to uncover.

It was almost seven by the time she reached Insomnia's corporate office building. She punched the elevator button several times, and after an eternity it deposited her on the sixteenth floor. The doors were locked, so she used the key card Alex had given her in case Kim ever decided not to let her in.

The suite was dark except for remnants of sun that trickled in through the windows. Alex had already left. He hadn't known she was out and would probably wonder where she'd gone when he got home. She crept into his office and used his phone to leave a quick message at his condo telling him she'd be back soon. Then, after a quick search of the room revealed he may have found the shoes and taken them home with him, she left.

A noise from down the hall stopped her. She waited, hoping she was imagining things. But she heard it again. And again.

She looked around to make sure she was alone, then tiptoed across the lobby and through a corridor until she found herself in front of William's closed door. The lights were dimmed and the blinds closed. She bent close to the door and listened.

A giggle, followed by a man's voice.

Her stomach turned. This couldn't be happening.

But it was, and if she wanted to know the truth she had to find a way to see what was going on in there. She spotted a tiny gap between the bottom of the blinds and the windowsill, and she squatted down and took a peek.

What she saw drained her lungs of air. Across the room, a blonde girl of maybe seventeen sat on the edge of William's desk wearing a black lace bra. He stood in front of her, kissing her and fondling her chest. Jacey stumbled away from the window before she could witness anything worse.

Though she shut her eyes, the disgusting scene continued to play in her mind. She fought the urge to vomit and left the building as fast as she could, hailing another cab and directing it back to her apartment. It wouldn't be hers in another twenty-four hours, because the final rent payment she'd scraped together had only gotten her through tomorrow. Maybe she could crash on Monica's couch after that, or she'd just sleep in her car. Any place free of emotional pain and dirty old men, things that had haunted her since she was a child.

She stepped inside and locked the door behind her, leaning against it and trying to catch her breath. Her chest still heaved and the contents of her stomach threatened to spill over. She poured a glass of water and sat down on her threadbare couch to examine what was left of her home. Most of her things had been packed, but since furniture didn't fit in her car, she would still have a bed to sleep in tonight.

For the first time in her life, the small room comforted her. In it, the high-class, messed-up world she'd been a part of for several days melted from existence. And for once, she preferred it that way.

Alex would never believe her if she told him what she'd discovered. And if he knew she wanted to make the information public, he would try to stop her. He would have to, to save his company. She had no choice but to avoid him until she figured out how to incriminate his pig of a father.

Chapter Ten

Alex examined his watch for the twentieth time in as many minutes. Nine o'clock. Where the hell was Jacey?

He rose from the sofa and paced in front of the living room windows, scanning the cluster of buildings and wondering if she was somewhere among the millions of tiny lights. Her message had stated she'd be back soon—two hours ago. He had no idea where she had called from or what she'd been doing, and he wished for the umpteenth time she would have stayed in the condo. Her restless roaming was bound to get them into trouble.

They hadn't spoken much since he had admitted to rigging the competition. He hadn't even mentioned that his promotion depended on her win—he thought she might have been flattered, or at least satisfied, that he was going to make sure she got the money regardless of whether or not she accepted the modeling contract. He would never do that for anyone else. But Jacey was so bent on doing everything herself, she refused to accept that his actions were meant to show how much he cared about her.

And now she was gone. A beautiful woman like her didn't need to wander the streets of downtown Miami alone. He would never forgive himself if something happened to her because he had agreed to do something he should have known would piss her off—and then he'd been crazy enough to tell her about it.

Growing more frustrated and worried by the second, he walked back to the kitchen phone and checked his voice mail again. The automated system announced that someone had called from the office—*his* office. Jacey's earlier message followed.

She had called from his desk phone?

He never paid attention to the numbers on his voice mail. He figured if it was important, the caller would leave a message. If he had known this earlier, he could have gone down to Insomnia and caught her there instead of spending the evening wondering where in the world she had gone. It figured that on the first day in six months he'd left work early, she would go there to look for him.

He would go crazy if he waited any longer. He had to go look for her, even if his search would be futile. He made a mental note—again—to get her a cell phone. How had people survived without those things? Then he headed for his car.

Jacey didn't have the money to go shopping or get her nails done or any of that girly stuff, so he could think of only one place to look. Holding his breath, he pulled into a parking spot behind her decrepit apartment building. She'd told him she had a couple of days left there, and sure enough, a light gleamed in her kitchen window. A thousand pounds lifted from his shoulders.

He shut off the engine and released a huge sigh. At least he'd found her.

When he reached her door, his first knock went unanswered, so he pounded harder. "Jacey, it's Alex. Open up, I know you're in there."

No answer.

Why was he chasing such a stubborn woman?

He raised his hand again. "Jacey!"

She opened the door.

The sight of her, in one piece and breathing, filled him with a sense of completeness he'd never experienced. He wanted to grab her, hold her to him and thank heaven she was safe. But then he remembered she had left him—quite deliberately, the way it looked—and decided she wouldn't welcome an embrace.

"I left my things at your place," she said, her voice void of emotion. "I'm sorry. I'll go get them while you're at work tomorrow."

Too overcome with concern to ask permission, he walked inside and closed the door behind him. "I told you I didn't want you to leave. I've been worried sick about you. Is something wrong?"

She waved a limp hand, concentrating on the worn fibers of her carpet. "Oh, don't worry about me. I'm fine. Why did you say your parents divorced again?"

"I never did say."

"Oh...right. Sorry." She sat on the couch, crossed her legs and chewed on a fingernail. She acted like he wasn't even there. What was wrong with her? And what did it have to do with his parents?

"It was typical," he explained loudly, since she didn't really seem to be listening. "He was a workaholic, and she never got any attention. Neither did I, for that matter. He was at the office at least fourteen hours a day, including weekends."

"I guess that's what it takes when you're the head of a thriving company," Jacey mused, staring into space.

"Well, maybe. But I wish my mother would have stuck around a little longer. Dad's retiring in a few weeks because of health problems, so he'll be at home a lot more."

Her gaze snapped up to meet his. Finally, he'd gotten her attention. "Health problems? What kind?"

"He's been having heart trouble. His doctor suggested that stress is the problem and he needs to get out of such a demanding position. So I guess I get to have the heart trouble now."

His laugh sounded only half-sincere, and he didn't like how close to the truth that statement was. His heart hurt already just from the way Jacey looked at him. Her expression formed a mixture of anger, hurt and confusion. He didn't know which part was directed at him or what he had done to cause it.

"Why the sudden interest in my parents?"

She shook her head and went into the kitchen to sip a half-empty glass of water. "I was thinking about what you told me last night. About your dad setting me up to win the competition. Do you think he does things like that a lot? Things that are kind of...not right? Selfish, I guess?"

Alex followed her and leaned on the counter. "I don't think so. I mean, he'll twist the rules to make a buck, that's for sure, but he doesn't hurt people."

He'd let success go to his head, but underneath that ego, his dad was a good person. Alex believed that. He had to. Otherwise, what legacy was he trying to save?

"He built Insomnia from the ground up, and I respect him for that. In that way, I've wanted to be like him my whole life."

Jacey coughed and put down her glass. "Wow. I had no idea."

"I don't really want to talk about my dad. I want you to come back to my place."

"That's nice of you, but I think I'll be fine on my own."

"You don't have a car."

She fidgeted, and he knew he had her. "I've been taking cabs."

"You can't afford that. And I have to withdraw my funds unless you're staying with me."

She blinked, looking hurt until she saw the smile playing on his lips. She managed a smirk. "I'm pretty sure that's blackmail."

"I can offer you some other benefits."

Desire sparked in her eyes. He took her hand and brushed his thumb over her knuckles. "I want you at home so I can be with you, not so I can take care of you. If you want, we can talk about whatever is bothering you."

She looked up at him, her eyes tired. "I don't really want to talk right now."

Her arms slid around his waist. He shivered at her surprising change of mood and placed a gentle kiss on her lips. "Come home with me."

"And we won't talk?"

"We won't talk."

She smiled. After turning off the lights and collecting her purse, she squeezed his hand and led him down the stairs.

But while he drove across town, she stared out the window in silence. Her troubled mood hadn't quite lifted. Alex skipped the exit for his condo and turned onto a side road, heading for a place that might cheer her up.

"Where are we going?"

"You'll see."

"Alex, I've had a bad day and I really am tired."

"Don't worry. This doesn't require any deep thought. Or talking."

She huffed at his teasing, but the corner of her mouth twitched upward. And when he pulled his car into the gravel parking area of a small playground, her eyes lit up.

"Are we going to swing?" Her hands clasped. She beamed at a thick metal bar with four plastic swings attached, sounding for all the world like a child visiting the park for the first time.

He chuckled. "Among other things."

She got out of the car and jogged across the tiny pebbles that covered the ground beneath the playground equipment. She sat on a swing and grinned at him, gesturing for him to take the one next to her. He obliged, though his body was much broader than hers and barely fit into the thing.

"My mom used to bring me here when I was having a bad day," he said.

Jacey looked at him, her fingers wrapped around the chains suspending the swing. She swayed back and forth, just enough to make the hair around her face wave in the breeze and drive him crazy with desire.

"I've never been to a park."

"Never?"

She shook her head. "I mean, I guess I've been to one, because there was a playground at my elementary school. But I was never in the mood to play. So I didn't."

His heart twisted. What little kid had *never* been to a playground?

He reached up and curled his hand over hers, pushing both of them forward and back so their heels lifted off the

131

ground each time. Her blue eyes were wide, staring up at the full moon that, thankfully, provided enough light for this late-night trip.

He kissed her hand, enjoying her rare display of elation. She was even more beautiful when she was happy, and he wanted her to feel that way more often. "Is there anything else you'd like to do while we're here?"

She pressed her lips together and thought for a moment, then shot him a playful grin. "Yeah. Over there."

The slide. Of course. It had been his favorite as a child too.

"All right, but be careful," he chided. "That one might be too big for you to handle."

Her heap of curls bounced on her back as she hopped her way to the tallest slide in the park. "There's nothing here that's too big for me to handle," she called over her shoulder.

His groin tightened. He'd brought her there to cheer her up with a little innocent fun, but if her idea of fun was naughty, he wouldn't argue.

She climbed the ladder and perched on top of the yellow plastic slope. Alex positioned himself at the bottom.

"Go on, I'll catch you."

"Promise?"

He winked. She threw her arms in the air, squeezed her eyes shut and squealed all the way down.

Her laughter saturated the night air. He caught her in his arms and she lay back against the slide, catching her breath.

"That was awesome."

He leaned over and touched his lips to hers, feeling her chest heave with exhilaration.

"You're awesome," he whispered.

"I don't know how to thank you for this."

"Seeing that smile has been thanks enough."

She smiled even wider, then covered her mouth and giggled. "Look, now I'm all embarrassed."

"Don't be."

He kissed her again. The euphoric wave Jacey was riding rushed to her lower body. She wanted him—for the high he made her feel, for the unique ways he made her smile, for being so gorgeous and sexy and fun and perfect. Driven by a passion so strong she could barely contain it, she wrapped her arms and legs around his body and pulled him atop her on the slide.

He shoved his hands into her hair and devoured a spot of flesh behind her ear. "Are you sure you want to do this here?"

"*Yes.*"

When he released her neck, she was certain he'd left a mark. The thought of having him imprinted on her skin delighted her and sent her thrill level to a new extreme.

"Alex."

His mouth traced a moist path along her collarbone. "Mmm?"

"Make it rough."

He raised his head, one eyebrow flexed. "I'll hurt you."

"Impossible."

With a grunt, he pushed up her shirt and unfastened the front clasp of her bra. He took her nipple in his mouth, laving it to a tight point, then grazed it with his teeth and left her entire breast throbbing for more while he tended to the other one.

Words failed her under the influence of his mouth moving over her chest, so she made a squeaking sound and reached for his jeans, dying to know he felt the same urgency for their bodies to be naked and joined.

He did. When she opened his pants, his cock strained against his boxers, so she released it and massaged the hot length in her hand.

Alex pulled up from her breast. "Oh, Jacey."

His voice was no more than a sigh. She loved that she could make him want her enough to lose control. She curled her free hand around the back of his head, played with his dark hair and nipped at his neck. He moved out of her reach to remove her sandals, then tugged her zipper down and slipped one leg of her jeans and panties off, enough to bare her to his gaze and give him complete access to her body.

She sucked in a breath, intoxicated by the rush of being so exposed outside and the fever of knowing Alex was seconds away from making love to her in the middle of the park. She laid her head back on the plastic surface and exhaled into the star-sprinkled sky, so excited she'd probably come if he so much as breathed between her legs.

He put that theory to a fervid test when he summoned her to the edge of the slide and knelt to the ground. Lowering his head, he nudged her knees apart and consumed the very core of her. She gripped the sides of the slide and tried not to hyperventilate, but the continuous motion of his lips and tongue took the air right out of her.

She moaned. Just when she lingered on the edge of climax he slowed his caress. Warm liquid flowed from her as she melted in front of him.

"That's it," he murmured. With a loud cry, she begged him to finish what he'd started.

He tasted her once more, then dipped his finger into the softness he'd created and gently rubbed it over her tender, pulsing flesh.

A fierce orgasm charged through her body. Her hips arched off the slide. She shouted, squirmed, implored him to let her go, but he held tight to her thighs and stroked her again and again until the sensation crested and she thought she would explode.

At last, he rose, shoved his pants to his knees and sank into her with one quick plunge. The friction against her sensitized sex brought tears to her eyes. She let her legs fall open and took him as deeply as she could, just to feel the strength of his body pressing against her soul.

He lifted her knees up to rest over his shoulders. His breath skimmed her ear like silk. "You did say rough, right?"

"I knew you wouldn't let me down."

She clung to him. Her fingertips dug into his shoulders, her body lost in his, and her mind swam with memories of all the times they had done this before. He rocked hard against her, and she absorbed the rhythm of his thrusts, the moisture on his chest, the melody of his ragged breathing. She never wanted to forget any of it. His movements within her sparked a depth of emotion she wasn't used to, a feeling resembling *need*, and she tried hard to block the telltale drops that still burned behind her eyes.

She had spent so much of her life believing beauty was an adversity, something to hide and be ashamed of because people wouldn't hesitate to take advantage of it—or, like her mom, use it to *their* advantage. She'd hated men, hated sex, hated herself for allowing her and her mother to live such a lousy existence. But Alex made her feel worthy of a better life. He made her long for his touch when he was there, and smile at the mirror when he wasn't.

With Alex, she felt beautiful.

His arms contracted around her, and they shared a release that left them both limp. Gradually, the world came back into focus, the scenery around her proving they had just made love atop playground equipment. She'd never felt more alive.

Slowly, Alex withdrew from her body. He rubbed his hand over his face and smiled. "I hope I've made your day better."

Her day. The words doused her like a bucket of ice.

Images of that evening rushed to the front of her mind. William's office. The young girl. She didn't want to remember. She looked at Alex, pained at the thought of destroying his tender expression, his company, and possibly his life.

Not to mention his relationship with her.

But she had to tell him. How could she survive another day knowing what William was doing to those girls if she didn't do anything to stop it? She couldn't. She knew all too well how they would feel about themselves later.

Alex tucked his shirt back in and Jacey pulled on her jeans, shivering though the night was warm and humid. She took a breath. It was now or never, and never wasn't an option.

She touched his arm. "I need to talk to you about something."

"Of course. What's up?"

She couldn't get the words out. She waited until they had adjusted their clothes and ambled back to the car. He looked at her expectantly, and she blew out a puff of air.

"It's Insomnia. Your dad. There's something going on I think you need to know about."

"My dad? What is it?"

She swallowed, then forced it out. "I saw him with a model. In the office when I went to look for you."

He didn't answer right away. Resentment flashed in his eyes, but she wasn't sure if it was directed at her or his father.

"Are you sure?"

"Positive. I could never imagine something that awful."

He fidgeted, obviously uncomfortable discussing his father's sex life. "Well. I'm sorry you had to see that, but I don't know about *awful*. I agree it's not appropriate for the workplace, but if a grown man and woman want to—"

"Grown woman?" Her outrage bubbled to the surface, erasing the uncertainty she'd felt about revealing the truth. "These girls are still in high school. Some of them can't even drive yet, and you call them grown—"

"Wait." He stepped closer and put his hand on her arm, but it wasn't the soft touch she'd become accustomed to. His fingers were cold. And they pressed into her skin with too much force.

"Did you say high school? Where in the world did you get an idea like that?"

"I told you, I saw him. Today in the office."

"No. You didn't. You couldn't have. My father isn't the world's most righteous person, Jacey, but he is *not* a criminal. Or a pervert."

"Alex, please. I know it's hard for you to believe, but I need you to help me. We have to stop this from happening again."

He mumbled something and opened the passenger door. "Get in the car."

It didn't seem like the right time to argue, so she sat down and prayed they would get home safely, because he was weaving in and out of traffic like someone acting entirely on a volatile emotion. Rage, for instance.

Not good when behind the wheel of a speeding, two-ton vehicle.

"Look, I'm sorry, okay? Can we stop the car and talk about this calmly?"

He remained silent. And kept driving. She closed her eyes, opening them only when she felt the car lurch to a permanent stop.

They were back at her apartment complex. She thought of how close they had been thirty minutes earlier, and a thousand knives twisted in her heart.

Alex gripped the steering wheel and turned to face her. "I know you think you saw a young girl in my dad's office, but I can assure you she was just one of the twenty-somethings he likes to spend his time with. It's not that unusual in this business."

She opened her mouth to object, but he shook his head and kept talking. "I'm sorry you had to see that," he said again. "I'm sorry he couldn't work things out with my mother and decided to date the models, if that's what's going on. But that's personal business, Jacey, not public information. I know what you're thinking and I'm telling you now, don't do it. Don't ruin this company for me."

His tone softened, but that didn't make her feel any better. He didn't believe her. He was taking his father's side over hers without even hearing her out, and that only proved how wrong they were for each other. Any fleeting hope she'd ever had for them in the long-term dissolved.

His troubled brown eyes reflected so much she wanted to trust, so much she wanted to be a part of. But she couldn't ignore her wreck of a childhood home, all the dreams she still had to realize, and most importantly, the scene in William Vaughn's office. That had probably been going on for years— Alex's mother sitting at home while his dad "worked late" with seventeen-year-old girls. Is that what money and power did to a person? Would Alex end up the same way?

Not only did she have to avoid becoming her mother, but she had to avoid becoming *his* mother.

She didn't respond to his statement. She just kissed him on the cheek, then opened the door and got out of the car, making herself do the last thing she'd ever wanted to do.

Act like everything they had shared didn't matter.

"It's been fun, Alex. A lot of fun. But we both know we were meant for no-strings-attached sex. So let's just pretend that's what this was."

With that, she walked up the stairs and returned to her apartment, making sure her door was closed before she gave in to the need to sob.

Chapter Eleven

Danielle Valdez slouched in one of Monica's kitchen chairs like a convict about to receive her sentence. Jacey offered her a soda and a big smile, hoping one of those would put her mind at ease.

She exchanged a look with Monica, who lounged on the sofa and held a magazine, pretending not to listen. Then she sat next to Danielle. "You don't have to tell me anything you don't want to, okay? I just need as much evidence as I can get that William Vaughn is up to no good."

Danielle nodded, her expression sullen. "I got no problem seeing that pervert behind bars."

"Behind bars? Aren't these girls giving their consent?"

"Sure, but only because he tells them they'll be famous. And one of them was a sophomore."

Jacey closed her eyes. If Alex's father had seduced a fifteen-year-old, the situation was direr than she could have imagined.

She touched the hot rollers covering her head to test their temperature. Brushing off her objections, Monica had offered up her guest room until Jacey could afford a new apartment. Now she was playing hairstylist and makeup artist for the second round of the contest, which Jacey planned to show up to at the last minute. She had avoided Alex for a couple of days and intended to continue doing so until she could get the truth about his father—and until she could think about him without enduring a gut-wrenching sense of longing.

"A sophomore." She signaled to Monica that the rollers were ready to come out. "And you know these stories are true?"

Danielle took a slug of her soft drink. "Oh, yeah. The girls at school don't seem to mind, at first. All they can think about is how rich and famous they're gonna be when their pictures come out. They talk so casually about it, like it's no different than having lunch with him or something."

Oh, please. Jacey wasn't exactly an old maid, but she couldn't believe the cursory attitude so many kids had about sex these days. If only they knew how much they'd regret those meaningless stints later, after they met up with someone sincere and understood the power of genuine desire.

Stop thinking about Alex.

"Where can I find some of the prints from their photo shoots?"

"You can't. That's how I knew something was up. There are only a couple of people who actually had pictures published. The rest are still waiting to even have them taken."

Monica plugged in her curling iron and tugged at Jacey's hair with a comb. Jacey tried to wrap her mind around what she was hearing. Not only was William offering fame in exchange for sex, but he wasn't even delivering his half of the bargain. How would Alex react to the news that the powerful father he respected and admired was nothing more than a dirty old man?

Her heart clenched. She had already seen how he would react. He'd gone into complete denial.

The comb hit a snag, and she winced. "Have you ever had a direct conversation with him?"

Danielle hesitated. The nervous glance at her mother pretty much answered the question. Monica took her hand out of Jacey's curls and waved it in the air. "Tell her everything you know, honey. Busting this guy is important, and I'm not upset with you no matter what happened."

"Well...yeah, I have. After I got cut from the Sleepless Siren tryouts, I got an interview at Insomnia's office."

"William's office, to be exact," Monica cut in.

Dani sighed. "Yeah. I walked in there and he was sitting at his desk. He told me to sit down, and we small-talked for a minute. Then he came and squatted next to my chair and told me that if I did what he asked, he'd make it worth my while. He said the further he got with me, the more coverage I'd get in the next spread. Then he put his hand on my leg and that's when I left."

Above Jacey's head, Monica muttered a stream of colorful Spanish words.

A horrifying thought occurred to her. "I wonder if Kim knows about this."

"Who?" said Monica and Danielle at the same time.

"Kim Starr. Alex and William's assistant. She's the guard dog who sits outside their offices and checks everything that comes in and goes out. She would have to know something's going on."

Danielle shrugged. "I don't know. When I was there, that chick was always on the phone. Maybe she's too busy to notice."

Maybe. Or maybe she was too concerned with Alex's personal life to pay attention to her job. That woman should have noticed and put a stop to this trash a long time ago.

"I need your face, honey," Monica said.

Jacey turned to get her makeup done, being careful not to talk while Monica worked on her lips.

"Don't worry," she said when she got a chance to speak. "He's not getting away with this."

"What are you going to do?" Monica asked.

"I'm going to prove it. I'm going to collect all the proof I possibly can. Dani, do you think you could get your classmates to sign some sort of statement saying all these things happened?"

"Definitely. They're pretty pissed that they haven't gotten any photo shoots yet."

"Great. I need to show something like that to Alex. He's completely blind to this side of his father. He thinks William's a business genius and a huge success. But even if that's true..." Jacey shook her head.

She was going to give Alex a real reason to take over the company—a reason a hell of lot better than the one about rigging the contest in her favor. It made her even more furious to know that William had picked *her* as the winner. The pig probably wished he could get his hands on her too.

"Okay, Jace, we're done and just in time," Monica announced. She checked her watch. "Whoa. Maybe a little late. The show starts in—"

"Oh, no!" Jacey leapt from the chair. She had already noticed the time and she would have to bust her ass to get to the auditorium and get dressed before the show started.

"Thank you so much for the beauty treatment, and thank you, Danielle, for your honesty. I hate to rush out, but—"

Monica hugged her, being careful not to mess up her hair and makeup. "Totally understood, sweetie. Good luck."

"Thanks."

They waved goodbye, and Jacey disappeared out the door, thankful once again for her generous friends. She was borrowing Danielle's car, because she couldn't afford cabs and she wasn't about to take any more money from Alex. The only cash she'd accept from here on out was the prize money, which would finally get her into school and out of the pathetic soap opera that her life had always been.

She arrived at the auditorium at least half an hour later than she should have. By the time she reached the dressing room all the other girls were gone, and even Kim had left her makeshift desk. When she imagined Kim sitting at Insomnia each day and allowing William to seduce teenagers behind closed doors, she wanted to go into the audience and strangle the woman. Instead, she focused her energy on winning the contest—which she could do without Alex's help—and dug around in her locker for her costume.

It wasn't there.

She slapped her hand against the metal door. Insomnia staff members were supposed to sort out the lingerie each contestant selected and put it in the appropriate lockers. Some absentminded newbie had obviously screwed up her order.

What was she going to do? There wasn't a single piece of lingerie in her locker, and she couldn't exactly walk on stage naked. Although, this was "Too Hot to Handle" night—as kinky as she wanted to go without going all the way, Alex had said. She'd picked out a pretty hot little number, but since that was nowhere to be found, surely she could put something together with all the bits and pieces of costumes strewn around the dressing room.

The announcer introduced one of the contestants. All the other girls were backstage and wouldn't be returning, and she had about five people to go before it was her turn. Her eyes scanned the room.

A young intern walked by, on her way back from the private restroom. Jacey grabbed her as she passed.

"Hey, do you know anything about the placement of lingerie in the lockers?"

"I know a little, what's wrong?"

"Have you seen a black and white, sheer little thing with lace garter suspenders on it?"

The girl looked relieved. "Yeah, don't worry. Amber found it. She's got it on and it looks great."

Apparently thinking she'd been a great help, the intern sashayed back to the audience.

Amber Lynn. The brown-haired girl who had raised her suspicions long ago. She was always giggling with Kim and whispering to other contestants when she thought Jacey wasn't looking. That witch had stolen her outfit.

Jacey didn't know why. She didn't care. Somebody was trying to get her kicked out of the contest, with the note and photo sent to Alex, and now this. It had to be related. And if she knew anything, it was that she never let anyone bring her down, not anymore. Not since she was a sixteen-year-old fool who had sacked groceries and let the manager feel her up on a regular basis because she'd needed the money so badly.

She had let people take advantage of her in the past, but she'd long since learned that it never got her anywhere—no further than the next dead-end job or crappy apartment. She no longer had anything to lose. She'd take a little risk this round, because showing this girl up had just become as important as getting votes—although the idea forming in her mind would certainly rouse the interest of the audience.

While she was at it, she'd clear up Alex's problem with the crazy photographer too. She smiled. He might think he was saving her, but she'd prove he wasn't the only one with cunning and power in his corner.

Alex squirmed in his seat, watching model after model take the stage. He wasn't even seeing them. All he could think about was Jacey and how he hadn't seen her face since she'd left him in the car last week. They hadn't even talked, because she didn't have a phone and he doubted she would answer his call even if she had the option.

Next to him, Kim clapped heartily for every performance. She'd been giddy all night, and the mood hadn't rubbed off on him. He had no idea how Jacey had supported herself since they'd parted ways, and he hated that there wasn't anything he could do about it. But she was right—it would never work between them. Even if modeling wasn't her cup of tea, her dislike of the business didn't give her the right to accuse his father of having sex with minors.

He still couldn't believe such a thing had come out of her mouth. It was bad enough that his dad had disrespected his mother by hooking up with a model at all, especially one much younger than her. He had clearly fallen into the trap Alex already knew to steer clear of—women who feigned interest in a relationship to gain face time at Insomnia.

His father would do a lot for a bigger profit, but what Jacey had suggested was downright sick, and insulting. It damn near broke his heart that she thought so little of his family. He'd never forgive her if she spilled that rumor in public and ruined his company. Because it *would* be his company, very soon.

"Oh!" Kim gasped in his ear while she gawked at something on the stage. "Isn't that gorgeous? I love that one."

He looked into the spotlight and just about lost his dinner. Gliding across the stage was Amber Lynn Harris, the contestant who had come in second to Jacey after the first round. Her popularity with the crowd was apparent as they roared in approval.

But Alex didn't care about her popularity. He cared about the fact that Amber was seducing the audience in *Jacey's* lingerie—the ultra-sexy black-and-white lace corset she had picked out to wear.

How had this happened? Kim monitored every detail of the competition, and various staff members constantly checked the lockers and picked up the pieces of any emergency that might take place.

"How did their outfits get switched?" he demanded to his assistant.

She gave him a quizzical look. "Huh? Amber picked out that piece. She loves it."

Impossible. Alex had submitted the order for Jacey's clothing after listening to her rave about it once she'd seen it in the catalog. And when an outfit was chosen, the computer locked it up so no other contestant could pick the same thing. Which meant Amber had taken Jacey's lingerie at some point while they were getting dressed, and Jacey had nothing to wear.

Damn it. Jacey's turn was *next*.

There wasn't any time to get her a replacement costume. Either she wouldn't show, or she'd be in jeans and a T-shirt, and that definitely wouldn't get her any votes.

There was no way he'd get her into the final round now without raising suspicions. Absolutely no way.

He ran through a mental list of staff members working behind the scenes and considered who to fire, then prepared to run backstage and tell Jacey to leave and he'd make up some story for the public about an illness and a make-up performance or something.

But there wasn't time. Amber slinked off the stage to the tune of thousands of screaming fans. She'd probably just won the entire competition. He couldn't imagine what was going through Jacey's head right now.

Her name boomed over the loudspeaker. The audience cheered. The curtain opened.

The stage was empty.

His stomach revolted like he'd fed it undercooked meat. For the first time, he was clueless as to how to handle a company crisis, if this could be called such a thing. Maybe she had decided to bail. Maybe she was late because she'd found something else to put on. Maybe she would walk on stage...butt...naked.

Oh. My.

He might have believed they were the only two people in the room if his ears weren't ringing with the excited racket coming from the crowd.

So she wasn't *completely* naked. She wore a button-down white shirt—wide open—and a teeny, tiny thong which was nothing more than a plaid triangle covering *only* what the rules required that she cover. He recognized the clothes as her own, and the pasties on her nipples had probably come from Insomnia, though he had no idea when she'd gotten them.

She also sported a pair of glasses he'd never seen, which she tossed into the crowd. Then she released the bun in her hair and let loose her flowing blonde curls. She was the naughty schoolgirl taken to the extreme—a point proven when she lifted a pencil to her mouth and slid the end of it between her lips.

The audience went insane. Guys stood on their chairs and whistled. Chants of "Take it off!" made full use of the room's booming acoustics. He'd have to call security if she didn't end this performance soon.

But he could only sit there and stare. The woman had more balls than he did.

He should have expected that given an absurd situation, Jacey could come up with an even more absurd response. She was feisty, determined and so sizzling hot that her impromptu act had worked. He caught her eye and she winked at him. He had underestimated her ability to take care of herself.

When she'd discovered her outfit had been stolen, Jacey hadn't worried about the rules of the competition or how well she'd fit in with the rest of the contestants. A lifetime of feeling like an outcast had taught her to ignore social guidelines and do whatever worked for her. She knew her audience—namely young, horny males—and exactly what would inspire them to mark her name on the ballot. She'd surely insulted a few of the women and the haughty contestants' mothers gasping behind their hands, but they weren't the majority, and they didn't matter.

She would make the finals, and maybe even without his help. She'd bailed him out of an impossible situation. And all this time, he thought *he* had been playing the shining knight.

He was about to jump up and head backstage to kiss her, but before he could move, she was on his lap. While the crowd egged her on, she ran her palms over his shirt, then rested her hands on his belt buckle and stuck the pencil inside the top of his pants. Dozens of flashbulbs went off in the press section. She leapt back up to the stage and gave a majestic bow to the standing audience before she disappeared behind the curtain.

Okay, now they needed to talk.

With a mumbled excuse to Kim about using the men's room, he hurried to the dressing area. The other contestants had taken seats in the front row to watch the rest of the show, so Jacey was alone.

"What in the world was that?" he asked.

"What was what?" With a laugh, she ripped the pasties off and slipped her bra and the white shirt back on, then pulled on her jeans.

He tried not to watch while she undressed so easily in front of him. He failed.

"I'm not sure this is funny."

She saluted and pulled her mouth into a straight line. "Yes, sir. What is it you wanted to talk about?"

"You just announced our affair to the whole world."

"I did?"

"Maybe you were a little too wrapped up in your performance to notice, but a million reporters took pictures of that lap dance you just gave me."

She grinned. "I know. It's perfect. The whole thing was perfect."

Alex stared at her. Maybe she was crazy.

"What I did was put your ransom note writer out of business. Don't you get it? Our picture will be all over the place tomorrow because I intended it to be. Now everyone will know you were just a prop for my performance and that we have nothing to hide, because if we did I obviously wouldn't have been sitting on your lap in plain view of every reporter in the city."

She bounced a little, so happy she was with her plan. He watched her, stunned, then succumbed to the smile that pulled at the corners of his mouth. Jacey Cass was an amazing woman.

Kim blinked at the ceiling, then rolled over and stared at the clock for the hundredth time. Three-thirty. She hadn't gotten a wink of sleep.

Her plans to ruin Jacey Cass were not going well at all. Instead, they only seemed to bring Alex and Jacey closer together. She'd thought that having Amber steal Jacey's costume would be a surefire way to get Jacey booted from the competition. But instead, Blondie had hopped all over Alex right in front of the entire crowd—Insomnia staff, press, everyone. They obviously felt they had nothing to hide.

She had fired Robert after the tally of votes had concluded that Jacey would be making an appearance in the final round. What was the point of having a private investigator when everything she'd hired him to discover was now public information? She didn't need pictures anymore. They would be all over tomorrow's newspaper.

Next to her, William grunted and turned over. Kim looked at his bare back and down at her own nakedness, feeling strangely foolish. The initial thrill of sleeping with him had faded and she wondered why she was still helping him carry out his mysterious plan to boot Jacey from the contest. What exactly was she getting out of this? Revenge? A tear slid down her temple. Who was she kidding? Katelyn was gone, and taking some model out of the competition wouldn't bring her back. What if her sister could see her now? Would sleeping with the boss and plotting the downfall of an innocent contestant really honor her memory?

151

Kim got out of bed, not even bothering to stay quiet. William slept like a log. She pulled on her clothes in a fury, disgusted at the person she had become. This had never been about Katelyn. It had been about *her*—her resentment of Alex's disinterest and the low self-image she harbored after years of being surrounded by underwear models.

It was true she needed to keep her job, but William had never threatened her career. She had jumped into bed with him because for once, she'd wanted the upper hand at Insomnia and in her life. William's plan for Jacey had provided her with a perfect opportunity to enjoy some special treatment.

She shivered and rubbed her arms as she left his place and walked into the breezy night. She felt like a whore, and she dreaded the next round of the competition. William was not a patient or forgiving person. Between her walking out on him tonight and the Board's continuing threats to replace him, she could only imagine what a mess he would make of the finale.

Chapter Twelve

Wednesday evening, Alex swallowed his second glass of scotch and pushed the empty glass back onto the counter. He left the kitchen and stood in the middle of his living room, surveying the huge room with such scant furniture and high ceilings that every sound usually echoed off the walls. But tonight, the silence in his condo was deafening.

Jacey had, as promised, retrieved her belongings. In exchange, she had left the key he'd given her, the address where she was staying if he needed to contact her about the competition, and a profound sense of loneliness.

Even when he was a child and his father was never home, his mom had been there in the evenings to play a board game or bake cookies with him. Though she'd been silent and brooding whenever his father was around, she had always put on a cheerful face for Alex when they were alone.

Now he had no one, not his buddies who had become more and more distant as they had gotten married or moved out of town, not even a casual date to enjoy a few hours with. He considered hitting a club and finding someone to bring home and fill the void in his bed for a while, but he immediately nixed the idea. He couldn't imagine touching anyone but Jacey.

He hadn't seen her in almost a week, hadn't touched her in nearly two. The competition's finale was three days away, and after that, there was a good chance she'd be out of his life permanently. How had he stayed sane when he had seen her only once a year?

Well, there had been other women, and he'd recognized that even though Jacey intrigued him, they'd had an unspoken agreement that the party was all they were willing to share. They hadn't known each other. He hadn't known how badly he wanted her in his life on a regular basis.

Restless, he poured himself another drink and went into his home office. He flicked on his desk light and sat down, inspecting the sheets of drawing paper in front of him. He'd been working on his collection, but suddenly it didn't appeal to him at all. He crumpled his latest designs and tossed them in the waste can. He had a better idea.

Pencil in hand, he got to work. He squinted at the details, drops of sweat forming on his brow while he moved the lead across the paper with furious strokes, intent on finishing the vision in his head. And when he was done, his last drink untouched and his pencil no more than a dull nub, he held the sketch up and took in the beauty of his creation.

He'd drawn the most provocative bridal lingerie he'd ever seen. A pure white, thong-back teddy covered in intricate beading, featuring a plunging neckline and thigh-high stockings with matching detail. Put it on a bride sporting perfect hair and makeup, maybe a pearl necklace draped over her collarbone. Hot damn.

A scene played in his head, of carrying Jacey over the threshold of a fabulous hotel suite, letting her down next to the bed and unzipping her wedding dress until it fell to the floor, revealing the breathtaking discovery that she'd worn his signature design.

Oh, God. He dropped the sketch and leapt from the chair, running his hands over his hair and returning to the kitchen. How could he dream about marrying a woman who was barely speaking to him at the moment?

The more appropriate question was, why had he let her go in the first place? Why was she sleeping somewhere else, their relationship returning to one of nonchalance and distance, instead of safe and warm with him—and why had he let it happen?

He grabbed his mobile phone and looked up his favorite retreat. Jacey obviously wouldn't be working tomorrow and he could go in late. He punched the number and the woman managing the resort for the night, an older woman he was well-acquainted with because of his frequent solitary visits to her property, assured him that his bungalow would be available within the hour.

Adrenaline pumped through his body and he dressed and packed in record time. With one last look, he bid his lonely condo goodbye and closed the front door. There was somewhere else he needed to be tonight.

His heart rate had slowed considerably by the time he arrived at the address Jacey had given him. What if she wasn't there? What if she refused to leave with him? He'd been so emotionally driven by his plan, he hadn't thought it through very well at all.

His first question received a positive answer when she opened the door. He looked to the sky. *Thank you.*

"Hi, Jacey."

"Hi."

Her lips moved, but she didn't seem to know what else to say, so he put his plans into motion. "May I come in?"

After a brief pause during which he held his breath, she stepped aside and let him in. He was one step closer to the night of his dreams.

"How have you been?" He shifted his feet in the entryway, eager to get her away from the city and to a quiet, secluded place where they could forget about their problems and focus on each other.

"I've been good."

"This is a nice place."

"It's my friend Monica's. She's on a date right now."

Alex nodded, familiar with the name. He stepped closer and touched Jacey's hand. "I'm glad I'm not interrupting a ladies' night. I'd really like to show you something, if you can give me a few hours of your time."

She raised an eyebrow. "Show me what? Where is it?"

"This way."

Though she crinkled her nose with suspicion at the way he motioned out the open door, she followed him. Inside the car he cranked up the air conditioning, trying to dry the sweat on his forehead. He felt like he was on a first date with his dream woman, and he didn't want to blow it.

Several miles away from the lights and noise of Miami, Alex turned onto the private beach road he had come to associate with peace and quiet. It was the perfect place for a romantic getaway, but he had never brought a woman there. He had never met one he liked or trusted enough to bring to his personal hideout.

Until now.

He drove through the open wrought iron gate that signaled the entrance to the property. Jacey craned her neck to see the beach and the ocean that gently lapped right outside his window. He smiled. It was beautiful, a perfect match for her.

"Here we are," he announced, parking the car beside a cluster of palm trees.

She stepped onto the sandy ground and looked around, her eyes wide. He knew what she was feeling. He too had been awed by the beauty and serenity of the place the first time he'd visited. Seeing it all again through Jacey's eyes was no less impressive.

The house itself was one level, made of white stone with one exception—the wall that faced the ocean was glass from top to bottom. Lush tropical trees and plants surrounded it, so that even if the house weren't located on a private road, no one would be able to see inside. A whitewashed wooden deck started a path to the secluded beach area, steps away from the back door.

An image of the wedding dress flashed through his mind again. That spot on the beach, right next to the house...it was perfect.

He shook his head. He wasn't here to propose. He was here to show her that he truly cared for her and wanted to work things out.

Jacey wiped her forehead and released a puff of air into the humid night. She gazed longingly at the water. "I'd love to take a swim in that."

Alex waved his arm. "Go right ahead. That's what we're here for."

"To swim? There are plenty of pools in Miami."

"To do anything we want. With no one around to see it."

She mulled that over. "So this place is completely private?"

"Absolutely. The road is blocked off and there are no other houses on this stretch of beach. It's all ours."

"I didn't bring a swimsuit. I don't even own one. I've never had time for that kind of relaxation." The words seemed to stun her, as though she couldn't associate leisure with her life. "But I guess if no one's watching, it doesn't matter."

She took off her T-shirt and dropped it onto the sand. Alex cleared his throat, anticipating her plans and not about to stop her.

"I'm watching," he said.

She kicked off her sandals and unbuttoned her shorts. "So?"

"So you're right, then. It doesn't matter if you don't have a suit."

The denim material fell to the ground. "Right."

She turned and walked toward the beach, clad in a white cotton bra and matching bikini underwear. So simple. So damn sexy. Alex grunted and threw off his own shirt, his gaze glued to Jacey's silhouette. Outdoor lamps emitted soft amber light that made her body and the outline of the ocean visible in the dark night, and he followed her, keeping his distance so she could enjoy a moment where it seemed this peaceful haven belonged to her. If she craved relaxation, that's exactly what he would provide for her.

He looked away from the swaying palms that dotted the shoreline in time to see her reach around her back and unclasp her bra. It fell and tumbled in the breeze as she continued toward the water, and she slipped off the panties just as her toes touched the surf.

His mind raced with images of what he wanted to do in that water, but he vowed to keep his hands to himself. Jacey waded in further, and when she was waist-deep, she turned and grinned at him, her full, naked breasts bobbing up and down with each wave.

He swallowed.

He willed himself to be strong, even while his cock stirred in his shorts, which thankfully *were* made for swimming. If he didn't hold onto that garment like a lifeline, he'd end up inside her in no time at all.

"This feels amazing!" Jacey shouted over the sound of the crashing waves. "Come on, slowpoke!"

She waved him in. The cool wetness shocked his bare legs and much to his relief, calmed the hard-on that had grown more painful as he'd approached her.

Apparently she hadn't heard his resolution not to touch her yet, because the moment he got close enough for her to reach him, she curled her arms around his back and pressed her mouth to his. He closed his eyes while he savored the warm softness of her lips and the way her tongue played with his. Her nipples poked into his chest and he couldn't resist rubbing his fingers over one of them. She rewarded him with a moan and pushed her body closer.

"Alex," she murmured, "have you ever done it in the middle of the ocean?"

Sweet heaven, she was trying to kill him. He had failed at keeping his hands to himself, but he *would* keep his dick corralled—for now. He'd brought her here for a little romance that didn't have to include immediate sex.

Of course, if showing her a good time meant fulfilling her physical needs, he could find ways to do that.

"No, only in a hot tub," he answered.

She pulled her head out from his neck and smiled up at him. "Yeah, I remember that."

"I remember every night I've spent with you."

"Really? I thought a rich and powerful man like yourself would lose track of all those names."

She was teasing him, but it disturbed him to think he used to be that way, when he had first made a name for himself at Insomnia. Apparently his father was that way too, a thought that bothered him no matter who or how old the women were. Alex considered his father's crooked business ethics, and for the first time, he wasn't sure he wanted to be like him at all.

What would being Insomnia's CEO do to him? Would he spend every waking moment at the office, just like his father had while he was growing up? Would he break any rule to make more money and give in to the temptation of being surrounded by lingerie models?

He shivered, and Jacey rubbed his arms and shoulders, thinking he was cold. He welcomed the way she'd drawn his attention back to her.

"I would never lose track of your name, sweetie. In fact, if I think hard enough, I can probably recall every dirty little act we've ever done. And all the ones we haven't."

He slipped his hand between her thighs and put two fingers inside her. "Mmm. That's impressive," she said between gasps. "What haven't we done?"

"We'll save that discussion for later tonight. Let me tell you what I do remember. I know that you like this." He moved his fingers in and out of her body and used his thumb to play with her clit. She writhed against him, her grip tightening around his neck.

"I know you *really* like this." He grabbed her lower back to steady her and slipped a third finger inside. Buoyed by the water, she brought her legs up and wrapped them around his waist while she thrust forward.

Her nails dug into his back. When she came, varying expressions of ecstasy crossed her face. He loved giving her so much pleasure. She stood up straight and he picked her up again, her hair falling over one of his arms and her knees around the other. She laughed while he carried her back up to the beach, thinking they might need to go into the house—and the bed—sooner than he'd planned. But when he stepped out of the water, she wriggled out of his arms and faced him, tracing the damp hair on his chest.

"I want to do something for you," she said.

He looked at her body, naked and dripping with ocean water. "Babe, I think you just did."

Another laugh. She darted up to the deck and grabbed a beach towel from the provided stack. Then she returned and softly kissed him. "I want to make you feel good, the way you always do for me."

"Hmm. Don't think I can argue with that offer."

"You can't. Now strip and lay down."

"Jacey, there's a big bed inside the—"

"Shh. No talking. Ditch those shorts and lay down. On your stomach."

Intrigued, Alex did as she asked, carefully tucking his semi-erection beneath him before he lay on the white cloth. Jacey knelt beside him, tucking his shorts under his head for a makeshift pillow.

"Ever heard of erotic massage?" She placed her fingertips on his back.

He suppressed a groan. "Sounds like something I'd be interested in knowing more about. Are you an expert?"

"Sort of. My friend Monica taught me. She used to be a professional masseuse, and for a short time we made a business out of it."

"You've done this to a lot of men, then."

"Actually, you'd be surprised how many women came in. They didn't care who was doing it, they just wanted to feel good."

Alex reeled at the thought of Jacey's hands on a naked woman. "Damn. I'm sorry I missed that."

She smacked his leg before digging her palms into his thigh muscles and rubbing. "Please. It's not like I thought it was hot. It was just a paycheck to me. At least the women could hold a decent conversation. The men just wanted to know if a lap dance was included."

"Schmucks."

"Yep."

She fell silent and Alex let his head drop to the soft ground while he savored the motion of her hands. She made her way from his toes to his thighs, over his ass and all the way up to his shoulders. Then she instructed him to turn over.

He did, and while he took in the full moon that hung in the sky, the sounds of the waves bubbling against his feet, and Jacey sitting comfortably nude beside him, her skilled movements sending chills up and down his body, he doubted life could get any better.

Then she cradled his balls in the softness of her palm, and he knew that it could.

"Are you still with me?" She massaged him gently and circled his cock with her free hand.

He nodded. His mouth moved, but he wasn't sure if any sound came out. Afraid he was dreaming, he opened his eyes and saw her smile, felt her touch...felt himself lose control of his body.

"Jacey, I'm going to—"

"I know." She released him and bent down to replace the rhythm of her hand with the suction of her mouth. With a groan, he gave in to the ecstasy in a series of pulsing eruptions. When he came down from his release, she lay next to him on the beach, watching him.

"Did you like it?"

He chuckled, reaching out to play with her long curls. "I'll be surprised if you couldn't tell. Now tell me, what can I do for you?"

Chapter Thirteen

Jacey had never been so unashamed of her body. She and Alex had run around the beach like a couple of nudists, and now she stood on the deck and patted her damp hair with a towel. All those tourists had it wrong. Sunlight, crowds and constrictive swimsuits couldn't come close to the euphoria of playing naked on the beach at midnight as though no one else in the world existed.

No one except Alex.

He was down by the water, collecting their clothes from various spots on the sand. He'd unlocked the back door and told her to go inside and get comfortable, so she wrapped the towel around her and stepped into the house.

She sipped an incredulous breath. *Wow.*

Hardwood floors, leather furniture, glass-topped tables. It was an intimate cabin with an art deco touch, lit only by a crackling fire and soft moonlight.

"What do you think?"

She turned. Alex brought their clothes inside and shut the door.

"It's beautiful. It's unlike anything I've ever seen."

"That's exactly how I feel about you."

He stepped closer and offered her a single red rose. Stunned, she took it, inhaling its soothing scent. She would have expected a man with as much money as Alex to stuff the place floor-to-ceiling with bouquets of flowers, a stunt she would have found boastful and crass. But the single bud she held in her hand was as tender as the gesture itself.

"Alex..."

His eyes locked onto hers. "Anything."

"Make love to me in front of the fire. That's always been kind of a fantasy of mine."

His gaze shifted toward the gleaming logs. He cleared his throat. "It's not real. I hope that doesn't squash the fantasy."

She smiled. "As long as you're here, the fantasy is perfect."

They gathered a couple of pillows and a down comforter from the bedroom suite and arranged them on the floor next to the flickering light.

"Perfect," Jacey repeated, and they dropped their towels.

She felt a sense of otherworldliness standing in that room, Alex's bare skin against hers in the middle of the warmly lit house. They stood right in front of the wall of windows, but the sand and the ocean were all that could see the way he kissed her, right before he lay on the blanket and drew her down so she knelt atop him.

Her hair curtained around his face. He raised his finger and traced the outline of her lips. For a moment she stared at him, lost in his impassioned gaze and unsure what to think about the sentiment that rose in her chest, threatening to dampen her eyes right in front of him. She took a shaky breath and lowered her face to his neck, tasting the salt that lingered on his skin from their romp in the water.

His palms ran up and down the length of her back, making her shiver and igniting the flame deep inside her that had burned for him since the day they first met. She pressed her hips forward and trapped his cock against his abdomen. The hard length strained against her and when she was wet, she rocked back and forth against him, a sweet torture for both of them that left him begging for more.

"Jacey," he breathed. "Just put it inside you."

"Uh-uh," she teased. "I want to hear about all those nasty things we haven't done yet."

He nibbled her ear and coaxed her forward so he could suck on her nipples. She grabbed the back of his head.

"I said the things we *haven't* done. You already know that drives me crazy."

"Okay," he murmured, his face still buried between her breasts. Finally, he pulled back and kissed her on the mouth. "Sit on my face."

Her eyebrows flew up.

"You heard me." He tugged at her hips. "Bring your pussy here so I can taste it."

She swallowed, so turned on by his demand she could barely keep her balance while she inched her way up his body, until his hands grasped her bottom and the soft, wet stroke of his tongue landed right where he'd promised.

She had nothing to hold onto, so she arched back and steadied her hands on the floor between his legs, her hips shaking against the persistent motion of his lips and tongue. He licked her up and down, paused to suck on her clit, then did it all over again...oh, God. She shouted, more than once. She was going to die of ecstasy. The windows reflected a sight so erotic she nearly lost her balance. She couldn't stand it for another minute. She had to give as much to him as she was taking.

Abruptly, she turned to face the other direction, eliciting a grunt from him, but he wasted no time getting back to business when she settled down and took his cock in her hand. It was overwhelming, taking all of him in her mouth at the same time he kissed and stroked the most sensitive part of her. Could two people get any more intimate than this? Even when they'd had sex before, it hadn't seemed as powerful and all-consuming as the way they now touched each other. It was certainly nothing she could imagine doing with anyone else.

She chose not to spend any more time wondering what that might mean, because an orgasm rocked her to the core. Alex tugged her away before she could make him come. He sat up, buried his fingers in her hair and thrust his tongue into her mouth.

She could taste herself, could taste everything they had shared since he'd brought her to this place, and she responded fiercely, kissing him deeply for so long she couldn't breathe when they parted.

"I want you."

"Right here." He sounded equally breathless. He opened his legs and anchored himself to the floor, then motioned for her to sit on his lap, facing him. Slowly, she lowered her body onto his until he was inside her.

They rocked together, heat generating between them—the sweat on their bodies, their warm, mingled breaths. The mutual massage was almost too slow to bear, and she wouldn't have been surprised if steam began to rise around them.

Finally, she cried out in frustration, so high in a state of rapture she just wanted him to take her. Hard.

"Alex. I need more—faster—"

He didn't argue. She untangled her body from his, and a moment later he was above her, his first thrust a sweet reward for her twice-pleasured yet unsated sex, still swollen and aching for him to fill her.

And he did. He drove into her with a force even stronger than the night at the park when she'd begged him to do it roughly. She welcomed the sound of each stroke when their bodies met. The rhythm grew faster and harder, the sounds in the room louder and more unintelligible, until her hips arched and her head lifted from the floor. His hands moved to her back, and he held her close to him while they shared an intense release. Only when she started to come back down did she realize the racket she'd heard in the room had been their shouts and moans.

Her breathing slowed. Alex guided her back down to the comforter, brushed a strand of hair from her face and watched her intently.

"You're shaking."

She smiled, uncertain, like a vulnerable young girl after her first time. "Yeah. That was..."

"I know."

She was glad he knew, because she couldn't finish her sentence.

What seemed like hours later, she still lay awake. A wall clock ticked while she stared at Alex. He snored lightly beside her. They hadn't moved since the orgasm that had almost made her declare a love she had no business feeling.

Yet the words lingered on her tongue. *I love you.*

She touched his face. If only life could be that easy—so she could tell a man like Alex she loved him, he would love her back, and they'd ride off into the sunset. But she knew better. Even if she dared to entertain the notion of Alex wanting her enough to be his wife, his father's recently-exposed activities ruined everything. No way would she allow into her life another parent bound by a sick sexual obsession.

She trailed her fingers down his chest, struck that the beautiful act she'd shared with him could cause so much pain. With Alex, sex was tender, erotic and safe. With her mother and his father, and so many other men she'd known, it was vulgar and dangerous. The contrast bewildered her.

William Vaughn had founded Insomnia and still sat at the helm. With a loss of respect for him came a loss of respect for the company, and Jacey planned to cut all ties with the place once the competition ended. Though it saddened her to think about it, Alex was one of those ties.

But what if he wasn't?

"Jacey?"

She started. Alex's eyes were open and looking right at her. "Is everything okay, honey?"

She gnawed on her lip. Did she dare ask him the question that had popped into her mind?

If she wanted him for longer than the two days remaining until the last show, she did.

"I was thinking about you," she began.

He smiled and ruffled her hair. "I'm thinking about you too."

"I was wondering—" Oh, to hell with putting it nicely. "Have you ever considered finding another job?"

"At Insomnia?" His brows crinkled.

"No. Somewhere else."

He might as well have installed shutters on his eyelids, because that's how closed off his gaze became whenever she mentioned the company in a negative way.

His heavy sigh brushed a tuft of her hair. "Is this about my dad?"

"No. I mean, not necessarily."

He rolled over and rested on his elbow, looking down at her, but his gaze softened before she could feel intimidated. "I can't leave. I'm sorry. Let's enjoy the rest of our night, okay?"

End of discussion. His tone made that clear. She nodded and pushed the idea out of her head, instead choosing to savor what would probably be the last time they made love. It was the one thing they had always done well, the one thing they had always agreed on. If a future with Alex wasn't in the cards, she would squeeze every ounce of pleasure she could from the present.

Jacey woke up late Friday afternoon and smiled at the stinging between her legs that reminded her of the many hours Alex had spent inside her body. It was the sweetest pain she'd ever known.

He had dropped her off at Monica's yesterday, and though he had offered his condo to her again, she'd insisted she needed some girl time to prepare for Saturday's finale. In truth, she needed time to finish gathering evidence so she could bust his philandering father before he reaped the benefits—monetary and otherwise—of the competition's success.

She padded into the bright kitchen and lifted her hand to shield the glare of the morning sun, unable to stifle a yawn. They had slept maybe two hours Wednesday night, moving to the bedroom around three a.m. and waking up again at five to continue making love. By the time she'd arrived at the house yesterday it was way past breakfast, and she had been sleeping ever since.

She poured a glass of orange juice and then sifted through her mail, which thankfully had forwarded to the right place. She danced a little when she saw a letter from Alex's mother. It was the final piece of evidence that would prove William Vaughn was and had always been a pedophile. She moved to the living room and collapsed on the sofa, releasing a pent-up breath.

But as she read the feminine handwriting, the anticipation in her stomach turned to stone. She took a sip of orange juice and read the letter again, but nothing had changed except the bitter taste in her mouth.

Melanie Vaughn confirmed her ex-husband had chased young models during their marriage. She offered her apologies that the behavior was still going on and praised Jacey's efforts to stop it. But she also made it clear, very clear, that none of the witness testimony Jacey had collected would make a bit of difference in a courtroom.

Hearsay, the letter stated. It would be nothing more than a young girl's word against William's, and the girls wouldn't stand a chance against his high-profile lawyer. Her own experience during the divorce proceedings had proven that much. No, Melanie said, if Jacey wanted to catch William red-handed, she'd have to get her hands on tangible evidence that would demonstrate his illegal—not to mention immoral—behavior beyond a doubt.

So...what? She was supposed to send a girl to William's office with a video camera strapped to her chest? How would she get visual proof of his actions without being there herself?

The answer hit like a sledgehammer. If she couldn't take him to court, she could catch him in the act and turn him over to an outlet even worse than authorities—the press. But she would have to play the intended victim and get it on tape.

It was possible—she was already forming a plan—but the notion of allowing that man to touch her made her want to heave the contents of her stomach into the toilet for the rest of her life.

But then she thought of him putting his hands on Danielle. She thought of the venomous eyes of the man her mother had brought to her at fourteen years old and the way it felt when the creep in the store had touched her. She shivered. There was no way she could stand by and allow that to happen to other girls because she was too afraid to face William herself.

She reached for her phone, then cursed. It still didn't work. She dressed as fast as she could and drove to Monica's shop.

"Oh, honey," Monica said when Jacey revealed her plan. "Are you sure you want to do that? There's got to be an easier way."

Jacey squeezed the hand her friend offered. "I'm sure. Busting this guy will make every moment of misery worth it."

"And what about Alex? Does he know you want to send his dad to prison and put the company in jeopardy?"

She was trying to ignore the fact that Alex had anything to do with the situation at all. And hearing the consequences so bluntly didn't help. Alex wouldn't see the reasons behind her actions. He would only know she was responsible for locking his father up and destroying Insomnia's reputation.

Could she really throw his future away?

She looked at Danielle, who was spending a day off school stocking inventory and listening to the conversation with interest. Jacey's heart broke. She hated to cause Alex pain, but she had no choice. Alex was a big boy. He had solid career experience and enough self-confidence to carry him down a different path if Insomnia folded. But the girls wouldn't be so lucky. If they fell into William's trap, it would affect them forever.

"I tried to tell him," she said quietly. "He didn't believe me."

Monica shook her head. "Well, I can't totally blame him, poor guy. Imagine finding out something like that about your own dad. Must be a shock to the system."

Jacey turned to Danielle. "So, what do you think? Is it okay if I use your name since he'll remember having seen you at your interview a few days ago?"

Danielle picked up the phone at the front desk. "Kim might recognize your voice. I have a better idea."

Jacey watched in awe while Danielle spoke with total confidence. "I'd like to leave a message for Mr. Vaughn. This is Danielle Valdez. I've given his offer some thought, and I'd like to come in for a second interview."

Chapter Fourteen

The evening before the finale, Alex once again sat in his office chugging aspirin. He stared out the window. What would it be like to live as simply as the sea gulls that crowed and swooped over the sparkling bay? Surely they didn't worry over last-minute costume orders that hadn't arrived yet, advertisers who were dropping their accounts at Insomnia without explanation, or an assistant who seemed so distracted it would be a miracle if anything happened right tomorrow night.

Not that he could talk about being distracted. The workday was almost over and he hadn't accomplished a thing besides fantasizing about his favorite contestant. His night with Jacey had been nothing short of heavenly—until she had continued to press the issue of his father. She didn't understand how important it was that he take control of Insomnia. In fact, she wanted him to leave.

It had something to do with her independence and her fear of being controlled by someone more financially powerful, and while he respected that, he couldn't give up the company after all the time he'd spent preparing for this moment. His promotion was close enough to taste. Once he snagged it, she would see that he wouldn't treat her differently because of his title.

"Alex."

Kim opened his door a crack and poked her head inside. "Your mother is on line two."

She left before he could answer, but he'd swear she was blushing. He didn't know where her mind had been for the past couple of weeks, but it hadn't been anywhere near Insomnia's corporate office. She had even forgotten to initiate her daily flirting ritual, although he couldn't say he missed that.

Most likely, she was bogged down with organizing details for the competition's finale. He could certainly understand that.

He cleared his throat and picked up the phone. "Hey, Mom."

"Alex, honey. How are you?"

They spoke for a few minutes, and he evaded the inevitable question of whether he was seeing anyone. When he could no longer stand to think of his experience with Jacey at the beach house without being able to claim her as his, he changed the subject to what his mother really wanted to know.

"Mom, the big competition is tomorrow."

"So I've heard. I'm proud of you, honey. You've really made a name for yourself. That show has even made the news up here."

Alex cheered silently. Insomnia was making news in Orlando, a couple of hundred miles away, all because of his idea. He was close. So damn close.

"That's great news. I knew this would work, and Dad has promised me the promotion if it does. So as soon as they announce the winner—"

His mother laughed. "I believe in you, dear, but I wouldn't put too much stock in your father's promises."

"Don't worry, this one's in writing."

"Well, good. You know I've wanted you to have that company since the day you were born. And I want it now more than ever."

Alex chuckled, cradling the phone against his shoulder and pouring a sugar packet into what had to be his tenth cup of coffee. "Why's that?"

She didn't answer, and he stopped laughing. "Mom?"

She sighed. "Oh, it's nothing. I just have to admit, I'm anxious to see him pay for what he's done to all those girls."

For crying out loud, how long had his father been chasing the models without his knowledge? Everyone seemed to know it but him.

"I know he can't keep his pants on and I'm sorry for that, but it was all consensual. It's part of the business, I'm sure." A business he wasn't so certain he wanted to be a part of when another image of Jacey flashed through his head. Was he strong enough to resist the temptation? Was that what Jacey worried about and why she had asked him to quit?

"Consent doesn't matter in this case, I'm afraid."

He slammed his coffee mug onto his desk. Brown liquid splashed all over what was probably important paperwork, but he didn't give a damn about paperwork right then.

"What are you talking about? There isn't a model employed here who's under eighteen."

"Sweetie, please don't tell me you've been that naïve. You know your father and I had big problems."

He searched his desk for some antacid to accompany the pills he'd already taken. This conversation disturbed him. It was way too similar to one he'd had with Jacey.

"You had problems because he worked all the time. If it were anything else, you would have told me about it when you filed the divorce papers."

"I didn't want you to hate him, Alex. Besides, I don't think he went after the younger ones until long after our marriage ended. I didn't realize it was so bad until—"

She stopped. Alex waited, his breath caught in his throat.

"What?" he finally demanded. "Until when?"

His mother began speaking quickly, something she did when she didn't want to tell him the truth. "There are rumors going around that William's been offering some of the high school kids modeling jobs in exchange for—well, listen, honey, I don't want you to worry about this. You're doing the right thing and after tomorrow, Insomnia will belong to you. That's all that matters."

Alex couldn't believe what he was hearing. There was no doubt in his mind who had started the rumors...and if the gossip was widespread, that explained the sudden loss of advertising. He pictured Jacey again, but this time she was fully clothed and in big trouble. Damn her for not having a phone. He had to talk to her. Now.

"I have to go, Mom. I'll give you a call after the show."

He nearly crashed into Kim on his way out the door. "Alex, can I talk—?"

"Later."

She sounded concerned, but he brushed past her without a glance. The competition had dropped off his priority list in light of the madness Jacey had started with his father. He had to stop her. If her rumors went much further, they would destroy Insomnia before he'd spent a second as CEO. His mother's money, as well as his own and that of all the people who worked there, would be gone.

He knocked on her friend's door, but no one answered. Jacey's car was in the driveway, but that didn't mean much since it never ran. Having learned his lesson once, he called the office to see if she might have gone there looking for him, but no one answered there, either. Insomnia had already closed for the evening.

Where else would she be? He tried to recall the store Monica owned, but the name escaped him. It was in Bal Harbour, though, that much he knew. He jumped back in his car and headed that way, hoping he would recognize the shop when he saw it.

He did. It was hard to miss, with *Spice* hanging in sparkly block letters above the door and gaudily dressed mannequins winking at him from behind the glass. He walked inside. A bell signaled his entrance but there was no sign of Jacey in the room.

"Can I help you?"

Behind the register, a pretty older woman in a beaded minidress watched him expectantly. "Are you Monica?"

"The one and only."

Relief rushed out of his lungs. "Thank God. I'm looking for Jacey. Have you seen her?"

She blinked. "Oh, wow. You're Alex, aren't you? Alex Vaughn."

"Yes." He tapped his foot and tried to remain polite despite his frustration at how long this was taking. "Do you know where she is?"

Monica's mouth opened, concern in her expression. "What's wrong? Is she in trouble?"

"What? No. I mean, God, I hope not. I just need to talk to her. Please."

"Oh. Well, actually, she had a meeting with your dad. Something about the contest, I think." She checked her watch. "If you hurry, you might still catch her there."

Jacey was with his father? This was getting worse by the minute.

"Thank you." Within minutes, he was back on the highway speeding toward the office. He had a bad feeling that whatever Jacey and his father were discussing had nothing to do with business.

When William Vaughn walked into his office, he locked the door behind him. Jacey swallowed, praying for the courage to carry out her plan.

So far, everything had fallen into place. Kim had scheduled Danielle's interview for seven-thirty, long after Insomnia's staff had gone home. She'd explained over the phone that she would leave the door to the suite unlocked, confirming Jacey's suspicion that not only did she know about William's after-hours romps, but she helped him arrange them.

Kim had also said William would be back in the office around seven-fifteen, after a short break. Jacey had arrived early and set up a webcam, and all she had left to do was make him incriminate himself.

Whatever it takes. She hoped she was prepared to follow through with that vow.

"Ms. Valdez," William greeted her without turning around. "So happy you changed your...mind."

Surprise, but definitely not disappointment, crossed his face as he realized the woman in the chair was not Danielle Valdez. Jacey took a deep breath. Time to lie her ass off and make it good.

"Mr. Vaughn, I'm sorry. I'm a friend of Danielle's and I begged her to let me take her place at this interview. My name is—"

"I know who you are." A smile tugged at the corners of his mouth. He looked her up and down before taking his place behind his desk. "Jacey, isn't it? One of our top contenders for the Sleepless Siren contract."

Her face warmed. "Yes, well, I'm beginning to question my chances at winning. I really think I blew the last round. I don't think I have a chance at getting enough votes to win."

He chuckled. "Oh, I'm pretty sure you're wrong about that."

Ignoring his reference to the rigged contest, which she burned to tell him she was fully aware of, she plunged ahead with her scheme. "No, I'm quite worried, actually. I really need the money, and I'm wondering if there's another job available here at Insomnia. It doesn't have to be anything as big as cover model. Any gig will do."

Knowing that a respectable executive would tell her to take a hike before he'd offer her a backdoor way into such a lucrative business, she waited for the reaction so many young women had witnessed. But when he leaned forward in the chair and motioned for her to join him on the other side of the desk, her skin crawled.

Her heart pumped wildly. She rose from her chair and stepped around the desk, eyeing the tiny webcam Danielle had taught her to install. Its green light blinked in rapid succession to signal it was doing its job.

William ran his finger along the satin hem of the skirt Monica had loaned her. Jacey unclenched her fists and gave him a shy smile.

"You know, I might be able to come up with a spot for you in the catalog, but I'd hate to step on my son's toes. I think he fancies you quite a bit."

She wanted to slap that knowing smirk off his face. His snide gaze gave him away. He knew from past experience that nothing, not even a beloved boyfriend, would come between a pretty girl and her chance to be a model. Yet here he was, trying to play the noble one. Sick bastard.

"Oh, no, no," she said quickly, even as she thought of Alex and wished he were there to help her, wished he had believed her in the first place so she wouldn't be in this position. William's fingers roamed further up the skirt. Hard as Jacey tried to be strong, she was scared as hell.

But that didn't matter. What mattered was revealing his true personality before any more girls had their dreams, innocence, and self-worth crushed by this conniving, indecent man. No matter who his son was.

"I can assure you there is nothing serious going on between Alex and me," she continued. "He's a nice guy whom I've enjoyed knowing. But my priority here is getting a job."

William licked his lips like a lion preparing to feed. He took her hand and pulled her a step closer. Nausea collected in her throat.

"So you won't object, then, if I take a look at your features and decide what type of merchandise would best fit your body type."

She wanted to run from the room, but her feet betrayed her. "Um, of course not. I expect you would need to have that information."

He lifted her shirt and palmed her bare torso, and she was sure he would notice her skin was cold and clammy. She squeezed her eyes shut, thinking of the girls, of Danielle...of

Alex. Her mind screamed his name even though she had no idea what he was supposed to do about this. He'd been born to a disgrace just like she had. She almost laughed at the discovery that they had something so pathetic in common.

But any thought of laughter, even the sarcastic kind, fled her mind when William raised her blouse higher and ran his fingertips over her white bra. "This will never do," he mumbled. "You need something red or black. And much more revealing."

This time, she couldn't help but jolt away from his sickening touch. Flustered, she ran a hand through her hair and tried to come up with an excuse for her response, but William chuckled and made one up for her.

"Don't be nervous, Jacey. I won't hurt you. I'm flesh-and-blood man like anyone else. The only difference is, I have the ability to make you a rich woman."

Bingo. Now she was getting somewhere.

"Really?" She giggled coyly. "Are you making me an offer?"

He pulled her down so she sat on his lap, but at least her shirt was back in place. She could handle this. As long as he never again went near the places on her body she saved for Alex.

His hand skimmed the side of her torso again before trailing down her thigh. He stared at her chest. "You know, the fashion industry is so hung up on young models, teenagers even. But you...you've got curves unlike anything I've ever seen on the younger girls."

Though her hand felt like lead, she forced herself to place it on his shoulder. If he was horny enough, he'd forget about getting himself in trouble because he'd do anything to get into her pants.

"A sophisticated man like yourself, checking out the local teenagers? I find that hard to believe." She laughed, then pressed her lips together and fluttered her eyelids at him. "You could do so much better."

"One of the perks of the job, darlin'. I've got what they want, they've got what I want—call it a business transaction."

Jackpot.

The webcam winked at her. Momentarily, she felt the thrill of victory. Now to get the hell out of his office.

"Of course, they just get a quick lay and a picture on Insomnia's website. I can offer *you* much more. I can make you a star, Jacey. Forget the contest. Spend an hour with me and we'll talk about doing a whole spread for the catalog."

His arms clinched her waist, and she felt the sticky chill of his lips on her neck. Oh, shit. She'd planned to make him eat his words, but she hadn't planned her escape. She had figured he would make her some sort of obscene offer and she would ask for time to mull it over before hightailing out of there. Now, he had her in a hold she wasn't quite sure she could get out of. The man was strong.

She squirmed, but it was no use. She couldn't fight too much or she'd blow her cover before she could get the video to the press. Would she have to suffer through sex with this vile man in order to bring him down?

No. There had to be another way. His mouth continued its assault on her neck and he moved to release the zipper at the back of her skirt. She stared frantically toward the door. God—Alex—anybody—

But neither God nor Alex was coming to her rescue. She plastered one of her hands to the back of William's head with fake passion, then reached down with her free hand and started to tug one of Monica's stilettos off. If she moved fast enough, she could shove it in his eye or between his legs. At least those damn shoes would be good for something.

To her shock and relief, someone pounded on the door before she could spill any blood. She took advantage of William's surprise to jump off his lap and fix her skirt.

Alex's voice boomed. "Dad, open up. We need to talk."

Jacey tossed a disappointed look in William's direction, too happy to be free of his grasp to think about what she would say to Alex. "Guess we'll have to do this another time. Say, after the show?"

"Count on it. My personal limousine will be waiting."

He strode to the door, and she took great satisfaction in knowing that the only thing waiting for him after the contest would be his fate.

"Alex, come in. Miss Cass and I were just discussing her future with Insomnia."

Alex glowered at her, his expression dark as coal. "Her future?"

"Oh, yes. She's got great potential, don't you think?"

Jacey stood in the middle of the room and watched Alex, begged him with her eyes to see what had happened while she'd been in there alone with his father.

But he just glared. He wasn't getting her unspoken message.

Once more, he was taking his father's side.

She could see it in the horrified way he looked at her. Her clothes were rumpled from the near-fiasco in William's chair, but she would never have guessed Alex would take that to mean she truly *had* approached his father looking for a paycheck. He would never think that of her. He knew her better than that.

Didn't he?

No...he didn't. Because the look in his eyes was pure hate, and it was directed entirely at her.

"Never mind, Dad. We'll talk later. I have a lot to do before the contest."

"As do I," Jacey added quickly. "Thank you for your time, Mr. Vaughn."

"Any time. I look forward to working with you."

She raced to the elevator before he could follow her, hot on Alex's heels. He didn't speak to her, didn't even look at her.

"Alex—"

"No."

"Alex, please, I—"

"No."

She shook her head. "What do you mean, no? I can't talk to you?"

Finally he looked at her, a dark glare that seared her heart in two. "No, Jacey. You can't. Because you're no better than the models who took my mother's marriage and her company away from her. You're looking for money. I should have known. What else could you possibly want from me? I mean, from my father."

The elevator doors opened, and Alex rushed inside. Before she could go after him, his assistant appeared behind her and grabbed her arm.

"Jacey, I need to tell you something. It's an emergency."

"What is it? What's going on?" She tried to focus on Kim, but her gaze kept wandering to the closed doors where Alex had disappeared.

"The contest. It's rigged. Alex is going to—"

"I know. Alex told me. We've already agreed—"

"No, you don't know. Neither of you." Kim's eyes were wide. She glanced down the hallway, where William's door was closed once again. "It's not Alex who's rigging the contest. It's William. He's setting Alex up."

Finally, Jacey gave Kim her full attention. "Setting him up for what?"

"To look like he's the one who's been offering the models sex in exchange for career advancement. He's got pictures of you two. He's going to release them as soon as you win so it looks like Alex planned the whole thing all along."

Jacey narrowed her eyes. "How do you know that?"

"Because he asked me to keep you out of the competition." Kim looked down, her face red. "I was responsible for the tabloid threat and for Amber wearing your costume. It seems William knew that the more I tried to ruin things for you, the closer Alex would stick to you. And that's how he got his evidence, by having someone record your...um, relationship."

Briefly, Jacey thought of the park and the beach. Just what kind of photos had William secretly snapped? But more appalling was the idea of Alex being publicly humiliated and held accountable for crimes his father had committed.

"Why would he do such a thing?" she demanded. "He's got health problems. He needs Alex to run the company after he retires."

Kim shook her head. "He's not retiring. The health issues are a cover. The Board found out about the minors and they're forcing him into retirement to save the company's reputation. He's fighting it tooth and nail."

"He's setting his own son up to save his butt."

"Exactly. I'm so sorry, Jacey. I was stupid, and I was helping him, but it got out of hand and—"

"No time to worry about it now. Do one thing for me and we'll call it even."

Chapter Fifteen

It was here. The moment Alex had anticipated for years.

The finale of the Sleepless Siren competition was about to begin. At the end of the evening, while the news media were still present, his father would name him President and CEO of the company. He should have been thrilled. He should have been backstage helping with the demands of panicking contestants or at the entrance of the auditorium greeting guests and thanking them for supporting Insomnia. Instead, he was sulking.

The memory of Jacey in his father's office last night, her clothes rumpled and her face flushed with desire, was more than he could take. He'd been a fool to believe she was different from all those other women, the ones who jumped into bed with his father, intent on taking advantage of his money and power. The ones who had jumped into bed with *him* for the same reason. Clearly, she had been one of the same.

He should have seen it coming. He'd known from the first day he'd shown up at her apartment that she didn't have a dime to her name. Even if she hadn't meant to use him, she probably couldn't help it. He remembered from his younger days, before Insomnia's business had exploded, that a seemingly endless flow of income was hard to resist.

But then what would explain her insistence that she didn't want him to give her a job? Her anger when he had offered to get her out of the contract if that's what she wanted? He didn't know. All he knew was that she'd allowed his father to touch her, and he couldn't forgive either of them for that.

So he sat in a seat in the middle of the auditorium, ignoring the bustle around him, unable to go backstage and oversee his own project for fear of running into Jacey. Their time at the beach house played in his mind like an old movie reel. She was the most passionate woman he'd ever met, and one he'd be unlikely to meet again. Even the prospect of controlling Insomnia didn't quell his sadness at her sudden absence from his life.

His phone vibrated in his pocket, and he dug it out with a sigh. "Yeah," he answered without bothering to look at the caller ID.

"Alex, honey, come pick me up at the front door."

"Mom?" He straightened in the chair. "What are you doing here?"

"I came to see your big moment, of course. I hope you've saved me a seat."

"I'll be right there."

He rushed to the auditorium's huge double doors, where his mother waited patiently, dressed to the nines in an elegant black dress. He smiled. She had always been the one classy woman in his life.

They hugged. "Mom, you look fabulous. I can't believe you came all the way down here for this. What if you run into Dad?"

She waved her hand. "Something tells me he won't be here. Too busy with other things, I'm sure."

Alex tried to ignore the pang of hurt her words induced. She was right, though. His father wasn't the supportive type. He wouldn't have any interest in watching the competition unfold— only in reaping in the profits after it was over.

"He better be busy typing up my contract. This show has been a huge success."

He wished he felt as confident as he sounded. He wasn't quite sure what he'd do if his father didn't show up for the announcement of both the winner and his promotion. Jacey's idea about finding a job elsewhere didn't seem so farfetched when he considered that prospect.

His mother followed him to the front row and set her purse in a chair. "I'll just be glad to see him out of this business. He lost his affinity for it long ago. Forgot that the purpose was to make women feel good, not have them make *him* feel good."

Alex snorted. "I'm not sure he had much choice."

"What?"

"Come on, Mom. Surely you've seen the way these girls throw themselves at Dad—and me, and anyone with any decision-making power. They want to be rich and famous. They're looking for an in. It's not like he had to chase them down."

She gave him a derisive look he hadn't seen since he was a kid, like he hadn't listened when she'd told him to. "I'm afraid that's not entirely true, honey."

Before he could ask what she meant, she pressed a file full of paper against his chest.

He looked down and took it. "What's this?"

"I didn't want to tell you this until after the show, but there's another reason I'm here."

He opened the folder before she could continue. A sick feeling took hold of him as he flipped through copied pages of signatures and letters condemning his father. One phrase kept catching his eye—*East Bend High School*.

It couldn't be true. It absolutely could not be true.

"What the hell is this? What's going on?"

"Sweetie, I'm afraid your father *is* guilty of chasing some of them down. I tried to tell you. This is a copy of a petition from several of the high school girls he tried to seduce into a modeling contract that he never intended to fulfill. Unfortunately, with some of them, he succeeded. Your father's a troubled man. Like I said, he hit it big and completely forgot what's important."

Alex stared at the record of accusations, unable to digest the truth. But a small grain of hope sprung to life inside him. "You're taking this to court, right? To get back your part of Insomnia."

"No, honey, this isn't my doing. One of your contestants collected all of this information and I was hoping you could help me locate her after the show. I need to thank her for following through with this. She's saved a lot of girls."

His eyes dropped closed.

He recalled the story Jacey had told him about her childhood, about the pain of being ogled and groped by her mother's lovers. She had told him about his father that night at the park, and tried to discuss it again at the beach house.

He had refused to listen.

"I don't want anything from this company, Alex," his mom continued. "I'm perfectly happy now. All I've ever wanted is for you to inherit your fair share of it, and it looks like after tonight, you may very well have the entire thing. Jacey got him to confess on video and has already turned it over to the press, along with the signatures. It's only a matter of time before the law knocks on his door."

His lungs grew tight. He checked his watch. Only five minutes before the curtain opened.

"Mom, I need to—"

"I'm so sorry that you're hearing all this, baby. I know he's your father and you'll always love him, but—"

"No, I understand, Mom. I understand."

He understood that he had completely overestimated his father. Sure, the man was a business genius, but he had sacrificed his own integrity and the emotions of young girls to feed his own greed. Everything Jacey had tried to tell him had been true. And she hadn't allowed his father to touch her— she'd forced herself to make him do it so she could get unquestionable proof of his crimes.

Idiot. He had let his loyalty to Insomnia cloud his vision of reality as much as his father had. If his feet had been on the ground, he would have seen the warning signs stamped all over his dad, and he'd have chosen to listen to the woman he loved instead.

He loved Jacey. How could he have been blind to something so obvious? He stood, ready to rush backstage to find her, but the curtain opened. Back in his chair, he took a few breaths and glanced at the program. She was third this time. He could wait that long. As soon as she stepped offstage, he would go get her.

But the second performance came and went, the curtain opened one more time, and there was no sign of Jacey. No props, no music, just a blackness that matched the void in his heart.

Déjà vu washed over him. But this time, much more than the competition's results would be affected by her absence.

A hush fell over the audience. Then a chorus of murmurs. The emcee made a brief appearance to announce that Jacey was ill and wouldn't be competing tonight. Alex looked around, noticing the empty seat next to him. Where the hell was Kim? Why hadn't someone told him about this?

He kissed his mother on the cheek and bolted to the dressing area. Empty.

He searched the locker room, the showers, the makeup counters. Nothing but scattered jeans and shirts, and the scent of too much perfume. His forehead dropped to the side of a set of lockers.

"She's not here."

Alex raised his head and turned toward the source of the information he'd already figured out. Kim approached him, her expression dull.

"Where have you been? What do you know about Jacey?"

She handed him a mini CD in an orange case. "She said you can go to hell if you don't believe her after you watch this."

He suppressed a bittersweet smile. That sounded like something she would say.

"What is it?"

"A copy of the footage she got of your dad while she was in his office yesterday. She recorded him on a webcam and I retrieved the video after you two left. If you don't want to watch it on your own, his incriminating statements will be all over the news tonight."

He closed his eyes. It was over. His dad's life, Insomnia's reputation, his own career and his relationship with Jacey. Trashed.

"Yeah, I've heard all about that and I really need to apologize to her. Do you know where she is?"

"She said she was leaving. That was last night so I'm sure she's gone by now."

"Leaving? As in leaving town?" *Last night?*

Kim nodded.

Alex grabbed his hair and almost pulled it out. "Please handle the journalists when this is over. I have to see my mother off."

He ran from the room without waiting for an answer. Cheers and whistles from the auditorium floated out to the parking lot, but it didn't mean a thing. A couple of police cars and several news vans had gathered outside, probably thinking his father was in there. Later tonight, the scandal would be common knowledge, Insomnia's success and the entire competition nothing but a sour memory.

But somehow, despite his certain unemployment and the prospect of his father going to prison, finding Jacey was all he could think about.

"Thanks for letting me crash here for a few days."

Early Sunday morning, Jacey stuffed her nightclothes—the last of her meager belongings—into a suitcase and looked around Monica's tastefully decorated home. She'd planned on getting out of town last night before anyone discovered her absence from the competition, but Monica had insisted that she rest before the long flight to New York. Jacey had to admit, it had been a good idea. The past week's events had exhausted her.

Monica smiled and tied her hair in a ponytail. "No problem, hon. You look much better."

She looked in the mirror of Monica's master bathroom, where they both stood applying makeup. "I doubt that," she mumbled, noting the circles beneath her eyes. No amount of concealer could cover up the pain of losing Alex.

"You're going to be fine," Monica insisted. "Javier will take good care of you. He's preparing an office for you as we speak so you can start tomorrow. And don't even think about paying me back for the plane ticket. I owe you for taking care of Danielle the way you did."

"I don't have any background in accounting. I owe *you* for talking your cousin into taking me on."

"Honey, please. You're a math whiz. Every time you help Danielle with homework I sit by feeling like a complete idiot. Javier will kiss my feet for finding someone who actually keeps his books accurately."

"Yeah. I guess you're right."

Monica put down her lipstick and turned to her. "Are you all right? This is what you want, isn't it?"

She nodded. "It's what I want."

The job, at least, was what she wanted. It required the use of her mind instead of her body, and it was located in a city far away from Insomnia and her childhood home—two places she never wanted to see again. It was perfect.

Even as she tried to convince herself of that, the loneliness that had been building inside her since she woke up continued to grow. She didn't know how she would get by without her daily conversations with Monica and Danielle. And Alex.

Oh, Alex. She took a breath and released it slowly, her eyes dropping closed. Visions of his body filled her mind. His face, his gaze on her...

"Well, we should get going if we're going to make it to the airport on time."

She snapped to attention. "The airport. Right."

Monica picked up the suitcase with a lot more spunk than Jacey could muster. She didn't like to feel upset that Monica seemed to be rushing her out the door, when her friend was probably just happy that she was finally getting what she wanted from life.

At least, what she had always thought she wanted. Those dark eyes entered her mind again. She pushed the image away.

She took one last look around Monica's house before heading out the door and into the passenger side of her friend's BMW. She swallowed hard as they drove out of the city, her experiences and memories nothing more than a racing blur on the other side of the window pane. They passed the street where Alex had taken her to the park, and a lump rose in her throat. Then they turned onto the road that led to Alex's condo, and she nearly choked.

Monica shot her a concerned glance. "Sweetie, what's wrong?"

"Nothing. It's nothing. I mean, Alex lives out here. I didn't know this road went all the way out to the airport."

"You learn something new every day."

"Yeah." She certainly had. She'd learned it was possible to love a man so much that his absence caused physical pain.

Even as the thought entered her mind, she clutched at her chest. It hurt. She missed him like hell and she hadn't even left yet. Why did he have to react so badly the other day in his father's office? How could he believe she was so shallow, and why couldn't he see how much she cared?

"Honey." Monica touched her arm. "We're here."

Jacey sighed and reached for the door handle, preparing for the sights and sounds of approaching airplanes. But the view out the window revealed a tall building and a uniformed valet who opened her door. Monica popped the trunk, and the guy started removing her bags.

They were parked in front of Alex's place.

She whirled to face Monica, her frustration growing when she saw her friend's grin. "What are you doing? I'm going to miss my flight."

"There is no flight," said a deep voice beside her, and she turned. Alex stood next to the car.

Instinctively, she started to reach for the hand he offered, but then she remembered the way he had blown her off as a greedy tart looking for fame and fortune, and she withdrew her arm.

"I don't know what's going on, but I'm not interested." She tried to breathe steadily even while her heart galloped at his sudden nearness.

Alex continued to wait patiently, and Monica leaned toward her. "Get out of the car, Jacey," she whispered. "I refuse to take you anywhere else."

"You can't do this to me. All my things are packed up, and I—"

"You'll be fine. Go."

Jacey glared at her. "Fine. But we're not done with this."

Monica kept grinning, so she gave up and stepped out of the car while hope and anger collided inside her. What could Alex possibly want? Probably to offer his financial assistance yet again. She just couldn't make him understand that she didn't want it.

"Look, Alex, if this is about—"

He put a finger to his lips and led her by the elbow to the building's courtyard, dragging her suitcases behind him. They sat on a bench beneath a palm tree and he offered her a folded piece of paper.

A check.

She clenched her fists, certain that steam was about to blow from her ears. But before she could lay into him, he placed his hand over hers and said quietly, "You won."

Huh?

"What?"

"The contest. You won. This is your prize money."

"That's impossible. I wasn't even there last night."

He shrugged. "Apparently it didn't matter. There wasn't any rule that said people had to vote for a contestant who actually showed up. You made enough of an impression during the first two shows."

"You're insane. Have you forgotten that the contest was rigged?"

"No, it wasn't. When you didn't show, I didn't bother putting in votes for you. Not to mention that after my mother and Kim showed me the truth about my dad, I wouldn't have dreamed of carrying out his ridiculous plan."

"So you know it's true, then."

"Yes." He looked down, then straight into her eyes. "I'm so sorry, Jacey. I completely overreacted when I saw you in the office. I never thought my own father could be capable of such a thing."

"What happened to him last night?"

"He's being questioned, and authorities are searching his home and office for evidence. The press is having a field day.

That's all I know right now, and frankly, I'm not too interested in hearing anything else."

She squeezed his hand. "I'm sorry too, Alex. I never wanted to hurt you or the company. I just couldn't let that happen to Danielle or any of those girls."

"I know." He sighed. "Insomnia is closed for now. Obviously the contest and the modeling contract are moot, because there won't be any summer catalog. But I wanted to make sure you got the money. You earned it, Jacey. By yourself. Kim went back and counted votes and even without my help, you made it through each round. Congratulations."

She swallowed. She couldn't have cared less about the contract or the money.

"What are you going to do now?"

He pressed his lips together. "That depends."

"On what?"

"You."

She opened her mouth to object, but he kept talking. "With Insomnia out of commission, I need a job. Monica and I have decided to join forces and open a one-stop shop for women. Sexy clothes, sexy lingerie, all in one place. It'll be a hit."

"You've spoken with Monica?"

"We had a phone conversation last night while you were asleep. I was impressed with that dress you showed me, Jacey. Really impressed. I contacted her because I was looking for you, and then we came up with our plan to keep you here and talked about the business."

She nodded. "Wow. That's incredible. I'm so excited for you two."

But though she meant the words, her voice fell flat. She'd been counting on that job in New York, which apparently didn't exist. What was she going to do with her life now?

"That's an awfully dejected face for someone who just landed a job at Miami's hottest new boutique."

She gave him an odd look.

"We want to hire you. As a media assistant."

"Alex, I told you, I don't want—"

"I said *assistant*. Based on the experience you've had thus far, you're qualified. Don't go jumping to conclusions. We can't promote you to media planner until you get your degree."

He winked, and her eyes lit up. "Really?"

"Really, sweetheart, if that's how you want to spend your money. We wouldn't dream of handing you the job until you've earned it."

Her hands flew to her mouth. She could go to school, and then hold a position of authority doing something she had a talent for. Something she had earned. It was a dream.

No. This time, it was a *reality*. Finally.

"Oh, wow," she cried. "I don't know what to say. This is amazing."

Alex smiled. "Say you'll do it. And then come upstairs with me, because I have something to show you."

Jacey watched with anticipation as Alex put his hand to a sheet-covered canvas in the corner of his home office. When he removed the drape, she gasped at the intricate beauty of the bridal sketch he'd revealed.

"Oh, Alex. It's gorgeous."

He cleared his throat. "Thank you. It's going to be the centerpiece of our ad design when the new business gets started. Think you might want to model it for me?"

She laughed. "Yeah, right. I'll never step foot on a stage again."

"I didn't say anything about a stage. I was thinking this would be more appropriate for our honeymoon."

She stopped laughing. She brought her hand to her chest, her heart pumping at the fervor in his gaze. "What did you say?"

His familiar scent intoxicated her when he took her hand and pulled her close. "Marry me. Out at the beach house."

"I love the beach house." Her knees began to shake. The memories still took her breath away.

He smiled. "I know. We can live there if you want."

"You'd buy that place just for me?"

"I'll do anything for you."

Her phone chimed inside her purse. She stepped away from him and dug through the bag to find it. Only when she flipped it open did she realize it wasn't supposed to work.

"What the—?" She peered at the lit screen, where Alex's cell number popped up. With a sheepish grin, he held up his phone. Somehow, he'd managed to punch in her number while she was distracted with the drawing.

She tried to glare at him, but it was tough when she gratefully welcomed her return to the connected world. She'd been getting sick of driving everywhere.

"Alex, I know you did *not* pay my phone bill."

"I couldn't resist. I'm not about to spend the rest of my life chasing you down."

She tossed the phone aside and put her arms around his neck. "I thought we just established that I'll be spending the rest of *my* life in your bed. You won't have to look very far."

His brow lifted. "Is that a yes?"

"It's a hell, yes." She stroked his hair and brought his lips down to hers.

"Even better," he said before she kissed him.

They left his study and made their way to the bed, and when he was deeply inside her, he whispered how much he loved her. Jacey smiled, answering in kind and releasing all her doubts and fears. In spite of so many bad examples, they'd gotten their relationship right. Alex knew every part of her now, and still, she felt beautiful.

About the Author

Two-time Golden Heart® finalist Avery Beck has crafted compelling fiction since age five, when she played school with her best friend and sent home a "teacher's note" that got the poor girl in trouble.

It seems natural that her two passions, writing and studying relationships, have found an outlet in romance novels. She is fascinated with exploring the "something" that draws two people together, and she hopes to share with readers the humor, fun, drama, and best of all, joy of falling in love.

Avery writes short, sexy contemporaries and believes life is not complete without the pursuit of dreams and an intense roll in the hay...or wherever one feels inclined to roll.

To learn more about Avery, please visit www.averybeck.com or send an email to avery@averybeck.com.

One night of anonymous sex. Zero consequences.
At least, that was the plan.

Sexy by Design
© 2009 Avery Beck

Dumped for another woman, Bree Jamison buries her white-picket-fence dreams—and her naturally shy demeanor—for a contract job behind the scenes of an erotic cyberstore. Her new life comes with a sexy public persona, and a driving ambition to earn a permanent position with the company.

On the day she's prepared to present her best work, she's shocked to discover her future depends on impressing her only one-night stand. The one man who could blow her cover and ruin everything.

Evan climbed out of poverty with sarcasm on his tongue and a ring in his eyebrow. He can't believe the vixen in front of him is the same woman who fumbled her way through their single botched encounter. Her offer for a do-over is an opportunity he can't pass up, not only to secure his reputation, but to satisfy his curiosity about the one woman he couldn't please.

In a bedroom full of the company's products, fiery arguments lead to experimentation—and then to a passion that strips away their masks. In that vulnerable place, their troubled pasts collide, baring secrets that force Evan into a hard decision. And Bree back on the road to heartbreak…

Warning: This title contains hot sex complete with four-letter words and battery-operated devices, as well as a kinky to-do list and the world's most entertaining office job.

Available now in ebook and print from Samhain Publishing.

Enjoy the following excerpt from Sexy by Design...

Bree couldn't take the honest approach, not yet. They were barely treading friendly waters, and she couldn't lose the upper hand until she'd convinced him that his original impression of her had been way off-base.

"I can see I'll have to prove you wrong." Her fingers wrapped around the handle of her bottom drawer and pulled it out so hard the entire desk rattled. Inside lay a hefty collection of vibrators in different colors, textures, and sizes.

Evan looked down at the array of fake penises and threw his head back in amusement. Chuckling, he managed to say, "I'm afraid work-related devices don't count."

"You didn't say that. You said I'd never seen one."

"I amend my earlier statement. So you've seen one. But you've never *used* one."

He drew that word out like a long, slow lick on an ice cream cone. Bree-flavored ice cream. From behind those sultry eyelashes he watched her, daring her to be turned on by his proposition.

She wasn't merely turned on. She was a hungry lioness circling her cage, waiting for the door to open so she could burst out and devour a succulent piece of meat.

Yum.

She glanced at her office door to make sure it was closed. Time to put her seduction plan into action.

Swallowing hard, she reached into the drawer and retrieved a sizable blue cylinder. Her hand shook with nerves, so she squeezed her fingers around the thing more tightly. If she were going to refute his assumptions, she couldn't be afraid of a vibrator. She needed to act like she'd used one every day of her adult life. Like having a man watch her touch herself with one came as naturally as breathing.

A smile played on her lips. Letting a man watch *and* using a sex toy? She could knock two things off the list with this one simple act.

Simple. Right.

Her smile fading, she blew out a shaky breath and brushed the tip over her exposed shoulder, seeing Evan's mouth open just enough to let her know she had his interest. With excruciating slowness, she dragged the toy down her arm, making a U-turn at her wrist before bringing it back up and across her collarbone. She shivered at the cool, tingly trail it left on her skin and closed her eyes, wondering how she'd follow through with this show when she'd never even done it privately.

Before she got that far, Evan rolled his chair closer. Her eyes snapped open. His penetrating gaze fixed on her, he removed the device from her skin and held it tantalizingly in front of her face.

"What are you doing?" she objected.

He didn't answer, just turned it on with a single flick of his thumb. The purr of the tiny motor made her jump.

The way he stared at her made her feel naked even though she remained fully clothed. The room was nearly silent, the buzz of the fluorescent lights drowned out by the beat of her racing heart. She should have bashed his hand, should have bolted from the chair.

But she didn't.

"Don't touch me with that," she rasped. "Don't you dare."

Yet still she couldn't move. What was wrong with her? Evan's attempt to take control of the situation wasn't surprising, given his sky-high confidence level. But *enjoying* his power trip was not part of the plan.

"So." His breath caressed her neck as he dipped the pulsating tip into the top of her dress, grazing the cleft between her breasts. "Would you like a demonstration of what this thing is really used for?"

He looked down, and she knew he'd spotted her rigid nipples poking through the thin fabric of her outfit. Lovely. As cavalier as he was to begin with, she didn't want to reveal that, at the moment, her attraction to him was fueling her quest for sexual experience. Much as she hated to admit that, it was entirely, irrevocably true.

Her mind begged her to move away from him. *Your terms, remember?* But her body refused to listen. One more moment of his dizzying nearness, one more second of his warm breath grazing her skin just the way it had when he'd been inside her, and she would lose this battle. She'd be taking lessons from him instead of showing him what she could do.

So why did it feel so good?

An inkling of smugness in his smile, he moved the device down to her knee and began sliding it up the inside of her thigh. "I'll take that as a yes."

No, no, no!

"Evan—"

"Happy birthday!" The door flew open and the entire staff burst in, cake in tow. Snapping to attention, Bree watched in horror as the vibrator dropped from Evan's fingers and rolled underneath her desk. For once, he looked stunned as well. Thank God it was one of the quietest designs.

Her computer monitor hid their frolicking from view just long enough for them to compose themselves. Evan ran a hand through his dark hair, doing his best to appear casual. "Wow, you guys didn't have to do this."

Paula stepped up and hugged him. "Well, it's Friday afternoon and we could all use a break. Didn't want to ignore your big three-one." She turned to Bree. "Sorry I didn't warn you, but you two have been locked in here all day working on the site. I didn't want to interrupt and make anything look suspicious."

Bree smiled weakly. "No problem." If Paula only knew that *she* should have been the suspicious one.

They moved the party to the conference room, and Bree excused herself. The throbbing between her legs made it difficult to play social butterfly. She practically ran to the restroom. When she got there, she washed her hands under cold water and dabbed at her moist forehead with a paper towel.

What the hell was that? She glowered into the mirror. The idea was to prove she could be an assertive, sensual woman, not a submissive girl who'd let him do whatever he felt like doing to her. He already believed that, and she had just wiped away any progress they might have made on the path to understanding each other beyond their one-night stand.

Now she'd have to start over. You hate him, she insisted to her reflection. *You hate him.*

LaVergne, TN USA
29 August 2010
195058LV00013B/2/P